ONE
SMALL
SECRET

GIFT-WRAPPED ROMANCE

Enjoy all five romantic comedies in any order.

Cabin Crush by Kasey Stockton

Merry Kismet by Anneka Walker

Solo for the Season by Martha Keyes

One Small Secret by Esther Hatch

Jingle Bell Jilt by Mindy Burbidge Strunk

BOOKS BY ESTHER HATCH

HISTORICAL ROMANCE

Manor for Sale, Baron Included

The Earl's Hideaway, No Ladies Allowed

A Proper Scandal

A Proper Charade

A Proper Scoundrel

ONE SMALL SECRET

A GIFT-WRAPPED ROMANCE

ESTHER HATCH

To Mandy Biesinger, who finally gets to read one of my books without seeing its messiest draft first. All it took was two concussions, a car crash, and a dog attack to make it happen.

"The most important thing in anyone's life is to be giving something. The quality I can give is fun and joy and happiness. This is my gift."

—Ginger Rogers

CHAPTER
ONE

"Which floor?"

The well-dressed older man near the elevator keypad probably thinks he's asking a totally benign question. It would be if this was a normal day and I was an even slightly normal person.

I eye the button with a big fat 15 plastered on it at the very top of all the others. The executive floor. *My floor.* I give the man a tight smile. "Eleven."

By *next* Christmas my answer will be different. I didn't spend the last three years busting my butt in Vietnam to stay on the 11th floor.

I shift to the side to allow a few more people to shuffle in, and only then do I see him. There, on the elevator wall, is Ruben Palmer, encased in glass and looking like he owns the world in his latest *People* magazine cover. He's wearing a suit and tie, but he's pulling at the tie and his dark hair is mussed. He looks like he just got home from work and is ready to take whatever woman is waiting at home in his arms and ravish her.

That *can't* be office appropriate.

The woman next to me doesn't seem to mind, though. I glance around at the rest of the elevator, and sure enough, most of the women are taking in his cover like it's a perk of the job. A 401k match, fifty-percent discount on all Palmer Hotel stays, and some eye candy every day on your way to work.

Who wouldn't want to work at Palmer Hotels?

If only the lady next to me could have seen him in high school. He wasn't even that cool—at least not until his first magazine cover, anyway. But I'd always liked him. Our families have been close friends for generations, and I *love* his grandfather, but we live in different worlds now. Even when our families do get together for dinner, Ruben is usually in New York with a supermodel or handbag designer, the handbag designer being the most current trend.

I look away from Ruben's picture. So we used to be friends. We aren't anymore and it doesn't matter.

Isolation in Vietnam was supposed to break me—send me packing far away from Ruben so he could…I don't know…feel comfortable on the 15th floor without worry of his poor little schoolmate bringing up his less-than-glamorous beginnings? Whatever his reasons were, it didn't work. I spent the past three years managing the building and opening of the first ultra-luxury boutique hotel on Tuyen Lam Lake, and I didn't quit.

Take that, Ruben freaking Palmer. You and your 15th floor can suck it.

The elevator dings. "Excuse me." I push my way between two briefcases with an apologetic nod and step into the development office.

I paste on a professional, no-nonsense business face and take a deep breath. A woman I don't recognize looks up from the reception desk. "May I help you?" she asks.

"I'm Cadence Crane."

She blinks.

"I've just transferred from Da Lat." Her face is still cloudy. "The city near Tuyen Lam Lake in Vietnam."

Her face brightens. "Ah, yes, it's your first day. Welcome to

Rosco. We're excited to have you. I'm Sylvia Harcourt. I'll get your paperwork and show you to your desk."

I smile, but seriously? I've been part of the development team at Palmer Hotels for longer than this woman, and Rosco is my hometown. Together we walk through the door that leads to the office space. I almost stumble as I take in what used to be the development floor.

Everything has changed. The cubicles are gone, and so are the offices. Or rather, the office walls. They've been replaced with glass, letting the sunlight shine into the large, open space. Desks are scattered about with nothing separating one person's space from another's.

What happened here?

Sylvia leads me past several desks occupied by men and women I don't recognize. Only a few of them glance up as we walk by. I scan the room more intently. One man two rows away looks familiar—Christian Rasmussen. He'd asked me to dinner once, but I'd been too busy with work to accept. I try to catch his eye, but he doesn't look up.

Emily emailed me a year ago when she'd taken a job in Los Angeles, so I knew she would be gone. We'd known each other since middle school, and went to college in Spokane together for four years before returning to work at Palmer Hotels. The two of us had been inseparable, which, perhaps, accounted for the fact that no one here seemed more than vaguely familiar.

I squint my eyes and look again. Ah, Rebecca! She'd come to coffee with Emily and me a few times. She's busy typing away with headphones in her ears. Whoever came up with the crazy idea to have open offices probably thought it would lead to more talking and working together, but it only took me two minutes to realize that all it had done was force coworkers to erect their own invisible walls.

So, I know two people. Two people. I stuck it out for three years alone in a distant country with city officials who had considered it their life's mission to make erecting a hotel impossible just so I could impress Christian and Rebecca with my return?

Well, them and Mom. I will never be able to convince Mom that working anywhere except Palmer Hotels isn't a demotion. I could become president of an oil conglomerate or a partner at a huge law firm, and she would shake her head and say something like, *Oh, wasn't Palmer Hotels hiring?* Mom is the type of Rosco native that still thinks the sun rises on Palmer Hotels and no one in their right mind would want to work anywhere else.

So here I am, a glutton for punishment.

Sylvia points to an empty desk. It sits right next to one of the glass-walled offices. "Here you go. I hope you love living in Rosco. Small town, huge corporation. It really is the best of both worlds." She smiles as if she has just said the most brilliant thing in the world, and not a sentence I've heard on repeat since I was born. "Tomorrow at 10 am we'll introduce you to everyone at our team planning meeting." She gives me a friendly wave, then turns and heads toward her desk.

I sit, take a breath, pull my company laptop out of my bag, and snap it into the docking station. Time to get to work. I'm not going to get to the 15th floor by sitting around wishing Emily was still here.

Ruben Palmer may have been born to run the company that employed nearly half of Rosco, Washington's working population, but I am going to prove myself, just like I did in high school, in college, and in Vietnam. He might have wished Vietnam would break me and I would give up working for his company, but I'm back with more hands-on work experience than anyone else on the development team, and I already know where Palmer Hotels should build next. I open my folder containing my communications about the Laos location. I've been emailing the department about the Luang Prabang region for over a year, and now that I'm here, they are going to listen.

"Cadence?" Half an hour into work, I look up from my computer and find Christian smiling at me with that broad smile of his. His blond hair is short and styled to an inch of its life, but the precise style suits him. Maybe it's been way too long since I've been in a position to date, but he looks insanely good. Why did I refuse to go out with him again? "I knew you were coming back, but I missed you coming in. How was Vietnam?"

I flash him my best smile. Christian is the first person to recognize me, and even if he hadn't been young-Brad-Pitt-good-looking, I'd beam at him. "It was amazing. You should see the hotel."

"I've seen pictures online."

"They don't do it justice."

"Not as beautiful as our lake, though?"

I tip my head to one side, tap my pen to a paper on my desk, and bite my tongue about his choice of words. I guess five years in Rosco has Christian thinking he's a local. He'd better not call the lake *his* in front of Geraldine Forrester. She would skin his hide and remind him that no one gets to call it that without having lived here for more than forty years. Even though I hadn't been born when Ben Palmer poured the foundation on the first Palmer Hotel, my family is as local as they come. My grandpa was the one to buy Ben's land so he could afford to build the hotel in the first place. "Nothing is as beautiful as our lake."

"Have you been since you got back?"

"In the snow?" I shiver. I still can't quite feel one of my pinkie toes from my five-minute walk into work this morning. I really shouldn't have worn heels.

"I don't remember that stopping you before."

"That's because I used to be immune to the stabbing face pain that comes with below-freezing weather. The snow and wind managed to get a lot colder while I was gone."

"Do you want help toughening up?" Christian raises an

eyebrow. Christian isn't asking me out, exactly. But he isn't *not* asking me out, either.

The thought of the short hike from the hotel to the lake makes goosebumps rise on my arms. But it's the most beautiful place in the world. Ben knew what he was doing when he built his first luxury hotel there, and Christian is literally the only person besides my mom who has acknowledged my return to Rosco. I shrug. "Maybe I do."

Christian's smile falters slightly, like I've completely caught him off guard. "Really?" His surprise and hopeful optimism seals the deal.

"Yes, really. When should we go? I'll make sure I bust out my old snow pants and mittens."

"Tomorrow after work?"

"Sounds great."

Christian's smile is broad enough that even Brad Pitt would have been proud. "Do you want to grab dinner first?"

Eating out in Rosco can be tricky. Before the hotel went up, there was one mom-and-pop restaurant, a bakery, a seedy bar, and a Zip's. With the influx of big spenders up on the mountain, the mom-and-pop restaurant started serving overpriced Italian cuisine, the bakery now imports all of its ingredients from France, and Zip's is still there for locals who wanted an inexpensive burger.

The seedy bar remains a seedy bar. Apparently hotel guests love the small-town feel of peeling paint and battered bar stools.

Not a single one of those options sounds like first date material. "I'll eat at home. Why don't you pick me up at seven? Are you okay with hiking in the dark?"

"I'm not sure you can call a boardwalk path to the lake a hike. We'll be fine, as long as you don't freeze."

I am one thousand percent going to freeze. But Christian's smile is contagious. "I'll wear extra layers."

All my extra layers. December in Washington is kicking my butt.

CHAPTER
TWO

I can't feel any of my toes by the time I reach my apartment building.

I'm not wearing my running shoes tomorrow, I'm wearing my insulated hiking boots.

I punch in the code to my first-floor apartment and throw open the door.

Someone jumps up from my sofa.

"What the—?" I bend down and rip one of my sharp-heeled shoes from my foot. It's in my hands faster than I thought possible and instead of backing out of the door and calling 911, I'm charging toward my intruder.

"Cadence!" She calls out, waving her hands in front of her face.

I squint my eyes. The last time I saw my stepsister, her hair was purple and she wore severe dark eyeliner, but the turn of her nose and the smattering of freckles on her skin is unmistakable. "Moira?"

Moira bites her lip and takes a few careful steps toward me. "Hey, Cadence. I heard you were back in town." She puts both hands up in a surrender pose. "Please don't stab me with your very scary looking shoe."

"But…" I take a moment to catch my breath, look at the shoe in my hand still poised threateningly above my head. Geez—what was I going to do with that? What if the person in my apartment had a gun? It's not like anything in here is worth dying for, or even getting much more than a scratch over. I've got to retrain my instincts. I drop my shoe and kick the other one off. "How did you get in?"

"Your mom is meeting me here later, so she gave me the address. Sorry I got here before you. I didn't realize you'd be working so late. Luckily for me, you still use good old 9653." She smirks slightly, and I narrow my eyes at her. It felt a bit too soon after being held at shoe point for her to be making fun of my high school passcode.

"So…" Where do we go from here? Moira and I barely know each other anymore. Our parents' marriage was a strange blip in my otherwise pretty idyllic high school years. "How long have you been in town?"

"Oh." Moira brushes some of her nearly black hair out of her eyes. It's styled in an edgy wolf cut framing her face. "I'm just passing through. But I wanted to see you and Ruth."

I can count on one hand the amount of times I've seen Moira since our parents' divorce. Heck, even the year we lived together under one roof I rarely saw her. Why did she want to see me and mom now? "Do you want a drink or anything? I have water or there might be some juice in the fridge."

"There isn't," Moira answers. "But I'm fine."

She'd been rummaging through my fridge? Typical. But she needs to eat—I can see it in the hollows under her eyes. They aren't as deep as the last time I saw her, but I would never begrudge Moira food. Her year with us was probably her only stable home environment in, like, forever.

"Dinner?" I ask, and she shakes her head no. "Are you sure? I'm making it anyway."

"No, really, I need to see your mom. But I wanted to see you first."

I walk to the fridge and pull it open. I have eggs and toast or…toast and eggs. Moira isn't missing out on much. I pull out the eggs and Moira sits at one of the four dining chairs. "How's life treating you lately, Cadence? Are you still chasing Ruben Palmer?"

I squeeze the egg in my hand. If it weren't for that one principle I vaguely remember learning about in physics, I'd be standing here with egg running between my fingers. I loosen my grip and try to calmly crack it on the counter. The egg smashes pretty much in half, but I manage to salvage most of it and drop it in the pan. "I am not, nor have I ever, chased Ruben Palmer. He has pretty much half of the women on earth in love with him, and I'm not adding my name to that list. He dated Alyssa Fourtuna when he was twenty-two. Alyssa Fourtuna. The lingerie model." I say it like there's a chance Moira doesn't know who I'm talking about.

Moira laughs deep in her throat. "I didn't mean chasing after him that way. You aren't stupid. And Alyssa Fourtuna is much more than just a lingerie model. She's a fashion icon. I meant career-wise. Do you still want to be more indispensable to the Palmer Hotel empire than he is?"

I smile, and I get the distinct feeling it may look the tiniest bit evil. Ruben isn't a terrible person, and it's not like I want actual harm to come to him. Most of our lives we'd been thick as thieves. First, because our families were so close. Later in high school we were always in the same group of friends, hanging out at his grandfather Ben's house all the time. I don't know if it's the fact that his family was put on the map while mine continued growing apples, but I've always liked beating him. After he sent me off to Vietnam without so much as a goodbye, beating him now would be that much sweeter. Moira smiles back at me, so I don't think she minds my twisted line of thinking. "Oh. Yeah. I actually do want that."

"It shouldn't be hard. All the man does is run around the country partying with models. When would he have time to actually work for the company? And his grandpa has a soft spot for you."

Is Moira the only other woman in the world who isn't blinded by Ruben's gloriousness? Why has she been hiding away for so many years? I could use a commiseration buddy where he's concerned. I try to be discreet as I glance at her eyes again. They don't seem bloodshot. She looks tired, but in a natural way, not like she's about to crash after using. "If he has such a soft spot for me, why didn't he stop Ruben from sending me to Vietnam?"

Moira smirks. "Fair point, but you should thank him for that." Moira's eyes get a far-off look. She'd always wanted to travel and make a name for herself in modeling or acting. I'm the one who wanted to stay in Rosco. Mom offered to let her finish high school here after her marriage with Garff fell apart, but Moira wanted to move on to the next place. And Garff wasn't about to be left alone after his third failed marriage. Moira leans forward in her chair. "What was it like?"

"In the big cities? Crowded." But the part of the country I spent most of my time in was different. Da Lat has its own culture built around beautiful hills, pine trees, and a train that only travels two stops. They even have cowboys. *Dalat Cowboys.* I smile. It was a sensational location. As always, Ben knew exactly what he was doing. And Tuyen Lake? Breathtaking. As much as I wanted to come home, I loved my time there.

"But not crowded by the resort?" Moira asks.

"No, not by the resort." That was the Palmers' way. Find hidden gems of breathtaking beauty and make them accessible to anyone with a few million dollars in the bank. Most of the locals in Rosco hated Ben for it. But I couldn't. Ben never forgot that it was only because of my grandfather buying Ben's orchards that he was able to start Palmer Hotels. And I see the beauty in what Ben does. There is something brilliant about searching out the world's most beautiful places and bringing them to light. Even though people criticize him for making his hotels only accessible to those who can pay through the nose to stay there, the exclusivity means keeping those nearly untouched places from becoming overrun.

"Well, I'm glad you're back. Sorry I broke in."

"You're lucky I didn't bring my pepper spray with me today. I didn't think I'd need it in Rosco."

Moira snorts. "Why would you need pepper spray when you have those fantastic heels?"

I laugh softly. "Next time, I'm shutting the door and calling 911. Or maybe you could give me a heads up."

"Sorry. It was cold outside, and I didn't have your number."

Mom had my number, but consideration of other people had never been Moira's strong suit. Her eyes flicker to my bedroom as if she's curious about the rest of the apartment.

"Would you like a tour?"

"No. I actually need to go. Your mom promised me some one-on-one time, but next time we should all get together." She stands up and grabs her purse.

"We should. But we better hurry, I'm sure some agency will be calling you to New York and you'll be off to catch your big break."

Something sparks in Moira's eyes. "You know me."

It's been so long since I've seen Moira's eyes light up with excitement. I can't even think of the last time. She's still extremely thin. Chasing the dream of becoming a model meant Moira had made certain of that, but this thinness looks healthier. Her face is still angular, but not sharp, and the hollows look artistic instead of sallow. Would I really see her again soon? Or was this to be it for another few years? Any goodbye could be a long goodbye with Moira.

Moira stands in front of me and sighs long and deep. Then she leans forward and gives me a hug. She was way too cool for hugs in high school. I wrap my arms around her, expecting a quick squeeze and release, but she holds me tighter than I expected.

When she releases me, her eyes are partially wet.

Maybe she'll be back soon. Maybe tomorrow we can have dinner together and catch up. Something has changed in Moira —something big. Maybe she's just grown up like we all have, but I think it's something more.

She turns with a wave and before I know it, she's gone.

CHAPTER
THREE

My eggs are rubbery and flavorless, but there's no way I'm getting off this chair and taking the four steps around the kitchen island to grab the salt shaker. My feet are still a little numb and prickly, and salt isn't good for me anyway. I need a grocery store run. I'm going to have to use Mom's car again. I'd gotten so used to not needing one in Vietnam, that for some reason I thought I would be able to get away with it in Rosco.

I'll call Mom tomorrow though. Tonight is all about pj's and curling up on the sofa to watch whatever 1990s rerun I can find. I can choke down eggs and toast for one more day.

I rub the back of my neck and hobble past the table to my bedroom. I push open my door and stop. There's a large, square, black bag, bedazzled with the image of Marylin Monroe, sitting at the foot of my bed.

What the heck? Did Moira snoop through my fridge *and* my bedroom? And how did she forget her bag?

I pull my phone out of my pocket, but I don't have her number. I try Mom instead. She doesn't pick up.

I text her.

> Moira left a blinged-up bag here. Can you tell her to come pick it up sometime tonight or tomorrow? And send me her number, please.

I bend down to grab her bag and I hear a soft squeak somewhere in the room. My heart stops. Did Moira let in a cat, or something? If there's a cat in the bed, I'll be freaking feral the next time I see her. The last thing I need is something depending on me for survival.

Sure enough, there's a lump on my bed near the pillows, and the blanket is moving. I shake my head and rub my eyes. Moira showing up is always bad news.

But when I get to the side of the bed, two round dark eyes are looking up at me and blinking, and they're not cat eyes.

I put a knuckle in my mouth to keep from screaming and then look back at the bag on the floor.

That bag...It isn't Moira's purse. It's a diaper bag.

And the lump in my bed is a baby. A freaking baby. This cannot be happening. Who stops by for the first time in years and leaves a baby? My hands start to shake and my cold toes are forgotten. How long is Moira going to be gone? She didn't say what she and mom were going to be up to, but her comment about it being just the two of them suddenly takes on more meaning.

Okay, maybe she needed a night off, and for some reason, didn't bother asking me if I was up to babysitting. But she never bothered to mention she was a mom. It's not like the baby is little. I'm not good at guessing, but I would think it's close to a year old.

I put my hand up like a stop sign in front of those blinking brown eyes as if telling the kid to wait, but that makes no sense at all. What's it going to do, stand up and walk away? I dial Mom again. It goes straight to voicemail.

The baby makes another squeak, but this time it's short and

its face scrunches together. I know that look. It's probably going to cry if I don't pick it up.

I take a deep breath. I'm not some monster. I like babies, don't I? A little bit, at least? And objectively, this one is a pretty cute one, with soft, dark curls. It's not the baby's fault that its mom is so stinking inconsiderate. I square up my shoulders. So I have a baby for an evening. I can handle that. I'll skewer Moira when she comes back, but I won't keel over and die.

I pull the covers down just as the squawking sounds turn into real cries. The baby is in a blue onesie and darker blue sweatpants. A boy? I scoop him up. He's way past the point of needing help with his head. I sling him to my side and bounce him on my hip.

The crying stops, and those big brown eyes stare at me like *I'm* the surprise.

"Well then, Mister. I don't know where your mama went. But you and I will have a pleasant evening. Let's just make one very serious deal. I won't call her any bad names if you don't throw up or poop on me. Okay?" He doesn't answer, but I'm going to hold him to it. "How do you feel about watching some TV?"

And that is what we do. After a few episodes, I get over the worst of my anger. The little guy isn't bad company. He doesn't complain about my choice of shows, and he hasn't even made a mess anywhere. I did have to change his diaper once, at which point I confirmed my suspicions that he was in fact male.

Five hours later, I'm cursing like a sailor. He's kept up his end of the deal, but I should have added that he also needed to sleep.

He's capable of sleep. He was asleep when Moira left him. What the heck am I doing wrong? I grit my teeth and swing him back and forth in my arms. Where is Moira? At what point should I comb the streets of town looking for her frozen corpse?

Mom's phone is still going to voicemail when I call. I've rocked him, fed him, cuddled him, but he just won't close his eyes and sleep. I drag the two of us into my bed, dump a bunch of pillows on his side of the floor so that, if he rolls over or tries to crawl off the bed, at least he'll have a soft landing.

He can crawl, by the way. He even toddles a bit, so I'm thinking that makes him more of a toddler than a baby. That *is* what makes a toddler a toddler, right? They toddle?

I put some lullabies on my phone and even though he's still awake, I close my eyes. Partway through the night I awaken with a foot in my face. I groan, tuck the foot under the covers, and fall asleep.

The next time he wakes me, he's crying. I glance at my phone. Three a.m. I grit my teeth and drag myself to the kitchen to make a bottle. When I get back to the room, I just hand it right to him. He can feed himself, so he's either advanced or perfectly normal —I don't even know—but thankfully, it means I can just go back to sleep.

When I jerk later, it isn't from crying or some random body part in my face. The sun is shining in my eyes through my curtainless window. I really need to make time to buy some blinds for my windows. I groan. What time is it?

I grab my phone from my nightstand and pound on the touchscreen with my thumb. Crap. It's dead. Note to self—don't play lullabies all night unless the phone is plugged in. If I ever decide to quit the hospitality business and write a baby how-to book, that will be chapter one. Work starts at 9 a.m. and the sun wasn't in my face when I woke up yesterday. I want to jump out of bed, but Moira's baby is still fast asleep, his face relaxed in guileless innocence. The devilish foot and wailing mouth are still, and he looks almost cherubic.

Cherubs are definitely overrated. Holding my breath, I slide carefully out of bed. I plug in my phone. I haven't slept past 7 a.m. in years. Please don't let this be the day I break that trend.

I run to the bathroom, turn on the sink, and splash water on my face. My mascara from yesterday drips down my cheeks. My hair is a disaster. I look like a raccoon who stuck its paw in a light socket.

My phone pings to life and I dash out of the bathroom and grab it. If Moira hasn't texted me yet, she's dead to me. I know people say blood is thicker than water, but she's only a stepsister, and a former one at that. We share no blood. We only lived together for one year, and she was a rotten teenager the entire time. I flip open my phone case and nearly drop the phone.

Bold white numbers flash 9:45. I'm epically late on my second day of work. Moira is for sure dead to me, because I'm going to kill her. I don't know her son's name. She left no instructions, no car seat or stroller. All I have is a diaper bag with enough formula for a few days and an even smaller supply of diapers.

No one has texted me.

I silently scream and dial Mom.

On the third ring she picks up. "Hel—"

"Mom, do you know where Moira is?"

"Of course I do. I dropped her off."

My heart is starting to do something weird. Moira had better be drunk off her butt, so she needed a ride from Mom. "Dropped her off where?"

"At the airport."

I pinch the bridge of my nose. What. Is. Happening. "Mom, why did Moira go to the airport?"

"She didn't tell you? I thought she went to see you last night. I picked her up right by your place."

"She told me nothing, but she did drop something off."

"Oh, that's sweet of her."

"No, Mom, it isn't sweet of her. Did you know she has a baby?"

There's a pause on the other end of the phone. "Moira?"

"Yes, Mom. Moira." Who else would I be talking about? "When was the last time you saw her before yesterday?"

"It's been two years, but I thought that was because she was waiting until she had good news for us. Yesterday she had the best of news, but..." Mom trails off. I can tell she's processing what I just said. "What do you mean, she has a baby? She didn't have the baby last night."

"That's because she left him here with me." I want to scream, but I'm keeping my voice down because the last thing I need is for him to wake up. Instead, my voice is all hissy and growling. "I don't even know his name."

"It's a boy?" Mom's voice goes watery.

"Yes, it's a boy, and I am going crazy calling him babe and little mister. When will Moira be back? And why wouldn't she have asked us about leaving him? Mom, you have to come over. I'm late, and it's only my second day."

"Cadence, you can't be late for work." Mom's voice is full of concern. Most of the old locals hate what Palmer Hotels did to our town, but Mom took her parents' love for Ben and his work to heart. Benjamin Palmer started the company thanks to their parents, and now it's our job to make sure Ben's legacy takes over the world. I grit my teeth. This isn't the time for me to get a lecture from Mom about what an honor it is to be working for Palmer Hotels.

"I know I need to get to work. I don't know if you heard what I said a minute ago, but *Moira left a baby in my bed*."

I hear the clinking of Mom grabbing her keys. "Why didn't you call sooner?"

I rub a hand down my face. "Your phone went straight to voicemail all night. Trust me, I tried. And without a car seat or a car, I couldn't drive him to your house, or I would have."

Mom is quiet for a beat. "Moira told me I shouldn't drive with my phone on—that it could be a distraction."

I raise my head to the heavens. "Yes, especially if your real daughter calls and tells you your stepdaughter left a baby in her house…without asking."

"I'll be right there."

Mom lives on the outskirts of town, on the land Grandpa bought from Ben, but Rosco is small and it typically only takes her fifteen minutes to get here. I throw on a skirt and tennis shoes. Today I'm packing my heels. I slick back my hair as quickly as possible and wipe off my makeup, reapplying it as well as I can with shaky hands.

Mom never told me where Moira went.

And more importantly, how long she would be gone.

I hear beeping at my front door. Mom is punching in the door code. I throw on my coat, grab my briefcase, give her a peck on the cheek and run out the door. Just before the door closes, I hear Mom make a cooing sound. She must have found the stinking little cherub.

I run north. The office is only three blocks from my apartment. Three blocks have never felt longer. But at least I'm not weaving in and out of people packed together in the Vietnamese heat. At least here I can sprint.

CHAPTER
FOUR

My running shoes squeak over the marble floors. I wave to the first floor receptionist and scan my badge for the elevator. No one else is waiting. Who would be, at 10:30? The conference room is on the 14th floor. I'm half an hour late for the planning meeting. Maybe I should go to my desk and pretend I forgot?

But then they might plan something without me. I didn't come back to the corporate office just to miss out on meetings that could shape future projects. I'm sick of my idea for the Luang Prabang region in Laos being ignored. I want a green light on this project even more than I wanted to sleep last night. I push the button for the 14th floor, tapping my foot as I wait.

No one gets fired for being late to one little meeting. I'll be laughing about this with Christian and Rebecca next week. Once I've proven how indispensable I am to the company, no one will care.

The door opens and I wave at a surprised receptionist and flash my badge. There are no open offices on the 14th floor. It's meant to be a show space with models of future and current projects scattered about the open floor. At the back is the main conference room—the first room I've seen that hasn't had its walls replaced with glass. Apparently large meetings are allowed privacy.

I crack open the door and see Mr. Auger sitting on the opposite side of the large, 40-person conference table. His eyes widen when he sees me. I look down at my watch and bite my lip. "Sorry." I mouth quietly. Luckily, there are several seats open right in front of the door. I sneak into one. I've probably long since missed my opportunity to be introduced.

I shrug out of my coat. The room is silent. Maybe they're waiting for me to give my excuse. Can't they just get on with whatever they were talking about?

I reach down for my briefcase and curse under my breath.

It isn't my briefcase.

It's Moira's flipping diaper bag, with Marilyn Monroe's sparkly face and all.

Could this day get any worse?

I look up and motion for everyone to continue, and only then do I notice who else is here.

First of all, this is no development planning meeting. Sure, Mr. Auger is here, but he's literally the lowest ranking person in the room. There are three VPs, the head of marketing, two women and one man I don't recognize, but based on the sharp style of their suits, they're probably not from the States.

I mutter another curse, and Mr. Auger motions with his head toward the door. The message is clear.

Get. Out.

I've stumbled upon a meeting way above my pay grade. I'm still sweating from my run, my hasty make-up has probably already worn off, and I'm wearing sneakers and carrying a black Marilyn Monroe bedazzled bag. I look so much like a joke, everyone here is probably quiet because they're waiting for the punchline. I give the three people I don't recognize a quick smile and then murmur, "Sorry, wrong meeting." I jump out of my chair and rush to the door without making eye contact with anyone else.

What are the chances I'll be laughing about *this* with Christian and Rebecca in a week?

About zero.

Because I'll never, ever tell anyone about it.

I reach for the door handle, but it's already swinging toward me. Before I can step away, the door hits me solidly on the forehead. A sharp jolt of pain makes my mind go blank and I stumble into the chair I'd forgotten to push back in. It spins and crashes into the table, Marilyn goes flying, and I land on my butt in a heap.

I curse much louder than I should in present company, and my hand flies to my forehead. If I'm bleeding it will be the perfect end to my morning.

"What the—?" A deep voice that I instantly recognize echoes in my ringing ears. Of course *he* would be the one stepping into the conference room.

I look at my hand. No blood. At least there's that. I take a deep, fortifying breath, look up, and a few more choice words cross my mind.

His dark hair is longer than it was three years ago. That isn't a surprise. I follow him on social media, and even if I didn't I would've still seen him on news platforms. It looks good on him. Everything always looks good on him. This day couldn't get worse.

Ruben.

But it does get worse. Ruben's eyes furrow and he looks with concern at my head. Then, probably after making the same assessment I did—no blood—his eyes drop from my face to Moira's bag, my disheveled shirt, and finally, my well-loved sneakers. He blinks a few times, then looks at the name badge hanging from my neck. "Ms. Crane."

He looked at my name badge? I went to high school with this man. We were on the debate team together, and I scored higher than him on speech every single time. I made out with his friend on his grandfather's couch, for heaven's sake. *Ms. Crane?*

"Sorry," I mumble. "I'm in the wrong room."

Wait. Why am *I* apologizing? *He's* the one who may have just given me a concussion.

He reaches for my arm, but then seems to think better of it. "Are you alright?"

"I'm fine. You barely bumped me."

No one will believe that statement with my bag, coat, and half my body sprawled about the floor. Ruben looks zero percent convinced, but there's no chance I'm staying in this room a moment longer. I grab my coat and leverage myself up with the chair. I'd hoped to make a name for myself returning to corporate. Well, the VPs are not likely to forget me now.

I bundle my coat close to my chest and reach for my bag. A can of Vienna sausages and a tube of some sort of ointment slipped out during the fall. I grab the sausages. Gross. I can't believe Moira feeds them to her child. Ruben reaches the ointment first. Subtle veins run along the top of his tan hand, and his fingers end in neatly trimmed nails. Even his hands are photograph-worthy. I remind myself that we used to be friends, so I really shouldn't hate him for that. But then I gasp when I finally notice what he's holding.

The tube is purple, and slashed across the top of it are the words: Extra Moisturizing Double Duty Rash Cream. He's looking at it like it's a Rubik's cube needing solving.

I snatch it out of his hand and toss it in Marilyn Monroe with the disgusting sausages.

I need to get out of this room. I lunge toward the door, but Ruben is still propping it open with one foot, taking up half the doorway. There is no way I'm getting out of this room without him moving—not unless he wants me sliding past him and grazing his arms and chest as I go.

I bite my lip. He must see my predicament. But his eyes are on Marilyn, no doubt baffled not only by the sheer amount of tackiness, but the unsettling contents inside. I clear my throat softly. There's no way I am sliding my body past America's

Heartthrob. Because here's the thing. I'm not above admitting that with his olive skin, perfect floppy hair, and thick, dark eyebrows he is next level good looking. Nor am I denying the way he sometimes has this look in his eyes that draws people to him. But I'm one hundred percent blaming social media for the way my proximity radar goes off just because I'm within inches of him. His magnetism can't be all natural. It's propaganda and most of the world has been brainwashed by it. I pride myself in being less brainwashed than most, but I'm not sliding against that tailored white shirt and open suit jacket.

"Excuse me." My voice almost cracks and I'm not certain he heard me, but a second later he drags his eyes off my bag and steps into the room. I jump through the door and escape faster than a stingy hotel guest sliding past the concierge desk forty minutes after check-out time.

CHAPTER
FIVE

'm not surprised when Mr. Auger calls me into his office an hour later. Christian looks up in interest and I grimace at him. If I'd had my briefcase I would have been able to change my shoes, but instead, I'll have to go in looking almost as unpresentable as I was in the conference room. I throw back my shoulders and march toward his glass office.

"What's going on?" Christian mouths as I walk by, but I just shrug. I'm not going to admit to the colossal mistake I made this morning. Not yet. Probably not ever.

I shut the door behind me. And for the first time, I think perhaps whoever designed the whole glass office thing hadn't been a complete idiot. If the conference room had been glass, I would have seen right away who was in it. Even if only the door had been glass, Ruben would've seen me and I wouldn't have this amazing goose egg on my head.

"I'm so sorry about this morning. I assumed the planning meeting was happening in the conference room. I was running late and didn't check."

Mr. Auger pushes his glasses further up his nose and squints his eyes at me. "You didn't get the email regarding the change?"

"No, sorry. I haven't seen it." I give him a nervous laugh. One

I've heard from too many lackluster employees, but not one I've never needed to use. "It's a funny story, actually. I grabbed the wrong—"

"Nothing about this situation is funny, Cadence," he says, with more ice than I've ever heard in his voice. Mr. Auger isn't the most reliable boss I've had. He's lost more than a few of my correspondences, including several about my Laos proposal, but he's always been extremely kind. "Do you know who was in that conference room?"

Unfortunately I did—at least, most of them. I nod.

"Then you must know how embarrassing it was for me to have to explain why *my* employee burst into the meeting looking like some teenager at a concert."

Mr. Auger's neck is reddening. I'd embarrassed him, in the type of meeting he probably didn't usually get invited to. Huge mistake. "I'm sorry. It won't happen again."

"It better not." He took a deep, fortifying breath and straightened, then morphed back into my cheerful boss. "Enough about that. I'm sorry if I came off as frustrated. I should have waited to talk to you until I'd had more time to brush it off, but I need the reports on possible new build locations that I asked you for yesterday."

I'd meant to work on those after I got home last night. "I can get you those this afternoon."

He tapped his pen on his desk. "I need them now."

I took a deep breath. "I don't have them."

"I hate to ask this, but could you skip lunch and get them to me as soon as possible?"

Skip lunch? He'd never asked me to skip lunch before. "The truth is, I've had quite the morning, and it seems I've left my laptop at home."

Mr. Auger went still. "What?"

"I slept in and was running late. I accidentally—"

"So, when you walked into that meeting you were only just

arriving at work?" He held up his hand. "You had your coat on, of course you were."

"My apartment is only a few blocks away. I can go and get my laptop now."

"No, don't worry about it. It sounds like you really have had a rough day. I'll have Christian do it."

I grit my teeth. I have never, ever had someone pick up the slack for me at work. "I really don't mind. I need to add a few things about the Laos location, and Christian hasn't been there. I'll have it done within two hours."

"Really, Cadence. Don't worry about it. Mr. Palmer told me I should ask you to go home at lunch and I was hoping to get them before you left. That's all."

"He told you what? Why?" But the dull ache in my head gives me a pretty solid clue. Did he feel bad about smacking me in the head with a door? "Because of this?" I point to my bump.

Mr. Auger shrugs. "Probably. Either that, or he doesn't want you running into our European visitors again." Oh. That is a distinct possibility. "I can have you look over the file when you get back to the office tomorrow and add what you deem necessary. For now, I'll have Christian finish it."

I open my mouth to protest. I haven't missed a day of work without giving months of notice in six years, and I could be back with my laptop within fifteen minutes. But I snap my mouth closed. I'm chalking this up as one more thing to blame on Moira. "I'll take a personal day."

I'm violently putting on my coat when Christian comes to my desk. His movie star teeth widen to a smile. "Going home to get your computer?"

"I'm going home, period. I should've done myself a huge favor and called in sick today."

"Are you sick? You don't look quite yourself, and not just because of that goose egg."

I pick up the Marilyn Monroe bag and all I can do is laugh.

"Well, I'm glad to hear that. I hope I don't look like I've had no sleep every day."

"Rough night?" Christian raises his eyebrows, obviously insinuating something personal, but if he thinks I can find a man to keep me up at night less than three days after moving here, he's pegged me wrong in so many ways.

"Yes." I tuck my chair into my desk. "I'll see you tomorrow."

"Not tonight? If you aren't up for the lake, maybe I could grab us some dinner?"

"No." I try to picture Christian showing up to my apartment with a baby crying in the background. I mean, there's a chance Moira will be back today, but if she went to the airport, most likely not. I'll probably have him for a week, minimum. If she would have asked me, I might have been able to take off work or find a sitter, but with no warning like this? She's made my life a living nightmare. "I'm sorry. Something very unexpected came up."

Christian's smile fades and his eyes change. I can see him sorting this rejection into the pile of those I gave him before I left. Make that one more thing Moira owes me—a date with a nice man, because I probably won't get another chance with Christian.

CHAPTER
SIX

Mom is some kind of baby whisperer. Moira's baby is sitting on the floor, Mom in front of him, making a spoon disappear and reappear behind her back. He's giggling like she's the most entertaining thing in the world. After all my singing, playing peek-a-boo, and trying to bribe him with tiny pieces of breath mints last night, he never once giggled for me.

Mom looks up. "You're home early."

"Yeah, well, work didn't go according to plan. I took the day off. Have you heard from Moira?"

"No, but it's the middle of the night there, so that's not surprising."

My hand freezes in the middle of reaching for my briefcase. "The middle of the night? Where is she?"

"She found a job opportunity. It's a three-month type of thing in Majorca." Mom smiles. "She's going to be on television."

"What?" My voice is loud enough that it makes the baby start and look up, his dark eyes wide and his lip trembling. I know that look. Any moment now, the tears will start. Great. Not only am I *not* a baby whisperer, I'm a baby terrifier. I lower my voice and paste a grin on my face. Babies can't tell when you're being insincere, can they? "Where's Majorca? Do you know if she's coming back for him?"

"Near Spain," Mom says and then her face falls. "I don't know her plans. She didn't even tell me about him. Why wouldn't she tell me about him? When Garff died I told her to come to me if she ever needed help. No one should be parentless in their twenties. I can't believe she's done this alone."

I do feel bad for Moira. Really, I do, but she has basically left her own child parentless and he is nowhere near twenty. "Moira has always had to do things her way. But what I really can't believe is how she didn't tell us anything about him. What if his father is looking for him? Is he even hers? We're stuck with this baby we know nothing about."

Mom drops her eyes and brushes a tiny curl on the top of the baby's head. "Moira isn't a kidnapper. She'll reach out. I just don't understand why she didn't include me in this. I would've happily taken him."

"Mom. What do you mean by that?"

Mom doesn't look up. "She didn't trust me with him. She gave him to you."

The truth hits me and I know exactly why Moira left him with me. It wasn't that Moira didn't trust Mom. She *knew* Mom would help her. "I'm the one she didn't trust, Mom. She had to drop the baby off with me, or I might not have helped at all." I unzip my briefcase and open my computer. "There'd better be an email from her."

And to my surprise, there is.

I motion for Mom to join me at the counter. She rushes over and we read together.

Cadence,

You've probably noticed by now that I left a piece of my heart behind with you. First of all, I want you to know how hard that was. It's been me and Axley against the world since the day he was born. I'm devastated to leave him behind. But I know you'll take good care of him, and I'm sure your mom will help too. Really, the two of you will do a much better job with him than I've done.

We've been moving around, chasing jobs that never last longer than a few weeks. But now I have a chance to do something that will put me on the map, and I have to take it. For both me and Axley. I'm going to be part of a new reality TV show called Billionaire or Broke? I'm pretty sure I got the job because I was the brokest person who applied. We're filming on the island of Majorca. Per my agreement with them, this is the last communication I can have with you until filming finishes in Spring.

Axley's father died of an overdose six months before Axley was born. It was terrible, but between that and my pregnancy I finally had the courage to get clean. Axley is my miracle in so many ways. Please take good care of him while I'm gone. I know you will.

And look for me on TV! Commercials should be airing soon. Show Axley his Mama on TV.

Moira

P.S. VERY IMPORTANT: I didn't tell anyone in the production company about Axley. At first I thought it was such a long shot that it wouldn't matter, and then as the process continued, I just didn't find the right time. If the press comes asking you questions, PLEASE don't tell them he's mine. I've signed all kinds of documents saying I'm free and clear and have no one relying on my income. Plus, you know how scandals at home play out on air—never very well. I'll deal with the fallout AFTER the show is done.

There's a brief moment of silence. Then Mom turns to me. "Axley? What kind of a name is Axley?"

She must be my mom, because that is *exactly* what I was thinking. "Mom." I shake my head even though I agree with her. "Does that even matter? She's left him with us for three months. We can't do this."

I sit at the table and hit reply.

Moira,

You cannot leave Axley with us for three months. If he's your miracle, you'd better hustle back here and get him. Mom and I can help you find a job—maybe here in Rosco, so we can all help each other out, but you cannot—I repeat, cannot—just leave him with us. Come. Home. Now.

He cried for you all last night.

I feel a little guilty about that last line, but Axley isn't my responsibility, and Mom is right. It's a ridiculous name. I type my name and hit send. An email immediately pops into my inbox.

Address Not Found

I curse and slam my laptop closed.

"Cadence, don't say that in front of the baby."

"I guarantee he's heard worse with Moira as his mother."

Mom rushes over to Axley and scoops him up. "Don't listen to your auntie. She doesn't know what she's talking about."

"We have no way to contact her. She didn't leave a number for the production company. We don't even know if the show is a scam. Maybe she's mixed up in some terrible human trafficking ring."

"She isn't." Mom huffed and pulled Axley closer to her chest. "She showed me her contract. She got a signing bonus and everything. Applied right on the company's website. Get that out of your mind."

"Which company?" I grab my phone out of my coat pocket. "I'll contact them now. Since she hasn't disclosed Axley, maybe they'll make her go home."

Mom grabs my arm, looks me in the eye and shakes her head. "Don't."

I throw my hands up in the air, cellphone clenched tight in my right hand. Is she serious? "Don't what?"

"Don't do it. You saw her. She's finally healthy. Happy even. And this is a dream opportunity for her. We can deal with the media finding out about Axley when she gets back. And then she will have some experience. She won't have to go back to those terrible temp jobs."

"You sound like you know what she's been doing for the past two years."

"I don't much, but I can imagine. Can't you?"

I make the mistake of looking down at Axley again. He's drooling all over my shirt, my spoon in his mouth. How has Moira managed on her own for the past year? It couldn't have been easy, especially without any support. "Why didn't she come to us sooner?"

"Would you have asked for help if you were in her position?"

I can't even imagine myself in such a position. But then, when we were teenagers, I don't think Moira would have imagined it either. She'd never really belonged in Rosco. She was going places. Unfortunately, she thought drugs were part of a rich and famous lifestyle and she started on those before finding the other two. With Axley's father dead, Moira wouldn't have had anyone. Where did Moira belong? There was only one place I could think of now...

With Axley.

Maybe Mom is right, and this TV opportunity will make a difference and put her in a better position to be with him.

I rub a palm over my forehead, only to feel a slash of pain from my bruise. I pull my hand away. "Fine, I won't call. Not today, anyway. But I'm not going to promise I never will."

Mom smiles. "One of us needs to head to the store. We need a car seat, a stroller, some more exciting toys than that spoon, and a lot more diapers and formula."

I close my eyes tightly. "I cannot believe I'm doing this."

"*We* are doing it. And it's going to be wonderful. I'll watch

Axley while you're at work, and then you can take care of him when you get home. It's only for three months. It'll work out. Moira should've asked us. She should've trusted that we would want to do this for her. But she wasn't wrong to leave him with us. We're going to have fun with that little bundle of joy, especially during the holidays."

Mom had a few really good points. I take a deep breath. "So, who's going to the store?"

Mom offers, which means it's my turn to see if I can make Axley giggle with a spoon as my only weapon.

Twenty minutes later, I'm still only getting smiles and a few grunts when my computer pings. I jump up. Maybe Moira has changed her mind. Maybe that's her saying she's on her way home.

But it's a message from Human Resources.

Ms. Crane,

Your relocation to the corporate office was done at your request, and was conditional upon three months of stellar record and engagement. It has come to the attention of our upper management that your performance thus far has been lacking. Among other things, you have been extremely late, interrupted an important meeting with potential investors, and failed to turn in reports in a timely manner. Therefore, we are terminating your contract in Rosco. You may return to Vietnam and assume your duties there, or you may look for employment elsewhere. Please inform us of your decision this week. Until that time, do not report to work.

Regards,

Stephanie Hansen

I grab the edge of the table, blink, and read the message again. I must have misunderstood. Return to Vietnam? As if it's around the corner, and this wouldn't mean uprooting my life twice in so many weeks? How is this happening? I was late one day. *One day.* Nobody gets fired for that. This has lawsuit written all over it.

But they aren't firing me. I read the letter a third time. It's the perfect brush off. I still have a job at Palmer Hotels, just in a different location. And while even that could be cause to contact an attorney, they were right—I'd requested the transfer. They never told me to move here.

I'm going to kill Ruben. It had to be him. Being late is not a reason for a consequence like this. This smacks of a personal grudge. And he has had one for me ever since my treetop hotel idea. One good idea from me and a lifetime of friendship went down the drain. He couldn't handle me in the office for two lousy days? Maybe seeing me brought back all the reasons he'd had for trucking me off to Vietnam in the first place. This sucks, because, sure, I was a bit competitive with him, but his family won the ultimate competition two generations ago when they became icons and mine acquired more apples.

He's already successful. He shouldn't be intimidated by an old friend who hasn't made it past the 11th floor. It's one thing to send me halfway across the world once, but now twice?

I hear a squawk behind me and my body goes limp.

I mutter a curse. I can't go to Vietnam. Not now. Not even if I wanted to. Mom can't care for a baby on her own. It was bad enough that she would have to do it for eight to nine hours every weekday. I sink to the floor and my mind goes numb.

What am I going to do?

A knock sounds at the door. Mom's arms must be too full to punch in the code, but I'm still in shock and can't manage to pick myself up. My phone is on the floor next to me, and I have a smart apartment. I tap the button that unlocks the door, and it makes a little dinging sound. Then I fall on my side and rest my head on the floor.

The door cracks open.

"Mom?" I call out in a desperate voice I probably haven't

used since I was 13 years old. But as the door widens, it isn't Mom standing there.

It's Christian.

His eyes widen as he takes in my dejected position on the floor. "Cadence, what happened? Are you sick?"

I groan and pull myself into a sitting position. I really don't want to deal with a coworker right now. Can't I just have one moment of dramatic self-pity to myself? Why is he even here? "I'm fine, Christian. I never should have out-debated Ruben Palmer in high school. That's all."

"What?" Christian's eyes furrow and he walks into the kitchen.

"Actually he was mostly fine in debate. It was the Redwoods treetop proposal. Too many people loved that one." Ben couldn't stop touting what a good idea it was, and I'd only been at corporate for six months.

Christian is standing above me, his gaze on my open laptop. "Hey." I lurch to a standing position. and reach for it. "That's personal," I say, but he pushes my arm to the side without looking up.

"You're going back to Vietnam?"

I groan but drop my hand away. "No. I can't."

"Then..." He turns to me but his face freezes when his eyes catch the other, smaller intruder behind me. "Who is that?" His words are slow and careful.

I shake my head, not in the mood to get into my whole life story with a coworker who soon won't even be that. "Axley."

His eyes widen and he looks back and forth between me and Axley. "Is he…a neighbor's kid?"

"No."

"Is he…" He tips his head to one side. "From your time in Vietnam?"

Axley has that stupid spoon back in his mouth and he's cooing at me. How will I answer all the questions? Can I say he's my nephew? How many people will hear about it if I do? As soon as anyone from town finds out, they'll know exactly who Axley is. The old-timers all knew Garff and Moira. And once her show starts airing, it will only be a matter of time before the media finds out.

How dedicated am I to protecting Moira's secrets?

I'm not sure, but Christian has intruded enough for one day.

"Yes, Christian." I tip my head and put a hand on my hip. I force heavy sarcasm into my voice. "He's a souvenir." He can draw his own conclusions until I get my story straight.

Christian doesn't smile or laugh, just slides his jaw to one side. "That's a strange souvenir. I collect shot glasses."

"Well, I collect babies, which is why I can't go back. One is plenty for the moment. Now, why are you here?"

"I was hoping to change your mind about going out. But..." He looks at the computer, then Axley, and then back to me. I'm one hot mess he had no idea he was stepping into when he opened that door. "Perhaps tonight isn't the night." He winces. "Unless, you need something?"

I shake my head. "That's kind of you. But...I think I need to figure some things out."

He nods like I've said something very wise. "I'm sure you're right."

Christian takes a few steps backwards. Great. Now he'll head back to work, tell everyone about me getting sacked, lying on the floor crying, and having a baby. If my apartment is so smart, why didn't it stop me from opening that door?

I've spent my whole life trying to prove my worth by excelling in everything I do. Look what it's gotten me. Ruben wouldn't treat a regular employee like this. There are protections in place against such things. But because he knows Mom loves his family, and heck—because I love his family, I could never sue them. I shake my head. No one should have that kind of power. At some point, I need to stop this competition and move on with my life. His family owns an amazing company and has become millionaires hundreds of times over. My family still owns an apple orchard. Big deal. My family *wants* to be apple farmers. Every single one of them.

Except me. But that doesn't mean I can only succeed at Palmer Hotels. I could go somewhere else.

Christian is nearly out the door but still facing me, looking hesitant. I raise my hand. "Actually, could you do one thing for me?" He stops, uncertainty flashing over his face. "If you see Ruben Palmer, will you tell him about Axley? Ask him how he feels about firing a woman with a child to support right before Christmas."

"If I see Ruben Palmer? When would I see Ruben Palmer?"

I shake my head. He's right. It's not like Ruben comes to the 11th floor for social calls. Not anymore. "You know what? Forget I said that. Life isn't fair. It's about time I learned that."

CHAPTER
SEVEN

've spent the last two days debating how I could ask for my job back. And there's no good answer.

I zip up Axley's new coat and pull the stroller Mom and I bought yesterday out of the closet. It's frigid, but I can't sit in the apartment for another minute. I'm used to working, and when I'm not working, either relaxing or having intelligent conversations with…well, anyone.

Thank you Axley and Moira for taking not only my job away from me, but my methods of coping with life as well.

I could talk to Ben. I haven't even seen him since I got back. But I shouldn't have to resort to using connections. I'm a good employee, and I know it.

I have enough savings to last a few months. My time in Vietnam was inexpensive and I'd gotten a raise before going. But if I don't want to use it all up watching Moira's baby, at some point I'll need to find another job. And if I want Mom's help with Axley, it will need to be in Rosco.

Even if I could pay for someone to help Mom so I could leave town, I have to admit, I've grown a little attached to the goober. I give him a wink and ruffle his soft curls. His hand shoots up and his chubby fingers grab mine. "We're going to stick around, aren't we?"

Which means everyone in Rosco will know I failed at Palmer Hotels.

But I didn't fail. I had one really bad day, for a really good reason.

There's a small part of me that hopes Christian will deliver my message and...what? That Ruben will feel terrible and offer me my job back?

Do I even want my job, if it's only mine because Ruben feels bad for me? No. I want him to want me there, not to pretend he doesn't know me and cart me back to Vietnam. His fame has turned him into some kind of narcissist. I'd suspected it when he first sent me to Vietnam, and this whole thing has confirmed it. I'm not good for his ego.

I unfold the stroller and strap Axley in. "Let's take your new wheels for a ride." He gurgles and bounces in the seat in response. It's definitely the cutest thing I've seen all week. Totally worth going out in the snow for.

I open my door, then roll him to the exterior door and kick it open. A gust of wind and snow envelopes me. Almost instantly my teeth start to chatter. Axley's eyes go wide and his body stiffens from the shock, but then he catches sight of the snow falling through the air and his excitement returns.

I narrow my eyes against the onslaught and turn to the left. There's just enough new snow on the sidewalk to make pushing the stroller nearly impossible, but it moves a few inches. I lean forward and laugh. I'm an idiot. The weather had been cold yesterday but at least it hadn't been storming. "Why in the world did I think we needed to get out in this?" I shout above the wind to Axley. His only response is to grab for another snowflake. Babies needed to be walked, didn't they? I mean, dogs get walked daily or they go crazy. If I didn't take him on a walk maybe he would start chewing up the sofa or something.

Or get jaundice. Babies who don't go outside get jaundice, right?

Maybe I should head to the bookstore and find a book on child rearing. Mom *seemed* to know what she was doing, but she hadn't mentioned jaundice even once. If she wasn't going to worry about things like that, maybe I should.

"Ms. Crane."

I crack an eye open further and look up. A black Porsche Macan is parked in front of my apartment building, and through the tinted, partially open window, Ruben is scrutinizing me and the stroller. What is he doing here? How does he even know where I live?

"Ms. Crane?" I holler back at him through the wind. What is with him and all this professional language? "Since when did you start calling me Ms. Crane? I crushed you in the third-grade spelling bee."

It might be the dusting of snow flying by me, but I think I see the corner of his mouth rise. "Get in the car."

I want to stick my tongue out at him so badly, but I also want to retain the smallest bit of dignity. Being an adult is lame. "This may be hard to believe, but I'm outside on purpose. I don't want…" I sneak a glance at Axley. "Anyone to get jaundice."

He slides his jaw to one side, then turns off the ignition and gets out.

He's wearing a long, thick, wool coat with a scarf that's probably made from some exotic animal textile, like baboon butt hair or something equally ridiculous. It's probably all the latest rage in Monaco, or wherever rich socialites hang out. He strides over to me, his athletic legs looking perfectly sculpted in his tailored trousers. It really isn't fair. I could look like a million bucks too, you know…if I had a million bucks.

The only thing my family has passed down to me are way too many apples. Well, that and now Moira's baby.

I look down at Axley in his Supercenter coat, and he tilts his head so he can stare back at me. I touch the tip of his already

43

pink nose. "We don't need designer clothes, do we, Axley? We're doing just fine."

The crunching of Ruben's footsteps come to a halt right next to me. "Can you please tell me what is going on?" His voice is low, like he doesn't want anyone to hear him. Not that anyone else is out on the street today. I glance up. Ruben's eyebrows are furrowed, his mouth a tight line. A thunderstorm is raging in the depths of his mahogany eyes.

I tip my head so he can see that I still think he's a little slow, even though he never was. "We're going on a walk."

"But..." He looks as if he's going to ask another question, then stops. For the first time since I found Axley in my bedroom, I am one hundred percent happy he's here. If nothing else, he's given me this moment. I have stunned Ruben Palmer speechless. He blinks a few times and looks up at my apartment building. Despite my valiant efforts, Axley and I have only made it a few feet. Mom should've bought him a sled instead of a stroller. "How's your head?"

I'd almost forgotten the way he banged me up on my second and final day at work. "It's fine."

"I felt terrible."

I don't respond, because of course he should feel terrible about it, and maybe if I wait long enough he will give me an actual apology about that and a few other things. Instead, he clears his throat. "I heard you were going back to Vietnam."

"Oh, you *heard* that, did you?" He arranged it. But the joke is on him. I'm not going to Vietnam, and he'll have to deal with the fact that I'm in his hometown, unemployed and destitute, thanks to his decision to try to get rid of me.

"You aren't?"

"No, we aren't going to Vietnam."

At the word "we," he glances at Axley again. He hasn't even asked me about him. Axley is one tiny burping elephant in the room.

"Christian Rasmussen cornered me after a town hall meeting and told me you had a child. I didn't believe him."

I narrow my eyes. "You don't think I could convince a man to have a child with me?"

A lightning bolt strikes in the thunderstorm behind his eyes. He leans over me and I'm bludgeoned by the one thing I never had a chance to compete with him on. He outgrew me in 6th grade and I never caught up. "I think you could convince a pole to have a child with you. I just thought you were focusing on your career."

He thinks what? I shake my head. Flattery is kind of his thing. Usually not towards me, but that doesn't mean he isn't capable of it. "Women don't have to do one or the other anymore, Ruben," I bite back, even though he had been perfectly correct about me. Christian wasn't the only man I'd turned down because of work. I did want to have a family someday, and if the right man came around I would have accepted a date, but thus far, no one had excited me more than whatever project I was working on.

He winced. "I know. I didn't mean..." He trails off, and I silently thank Moira again. If I'd known all I needed to do to make Ruben lose his cool was to have a baby, I might have considered doing it sooner.

I heave the stroller and it slides forward. Barely. I said I was going for a walk. If all I do is make it to the corner of the block and back, that's still a walk, isn't it? I push again, another inch.

Ruben's leather-gloved hands join mine on the stroller. His right arm crosses over my left, and his hand rests between mine. His other hand takes the outside edge on his side. His body heat blocks the wind, and suddenly my walk has become a lot more comfortable. But also, a lot less comfortable, in non-weather-related ways.

The stroller moves forward as if there's no snow on the side-walk. The stroller bar isn't exactly huge, so Ruben's legs and side are pressed against me. I try to keep my stride opposite of his to decrease the amount of touching going on, but our legs sliding past each other is too distracting, so after a few steps I match my stride to his. Every inch of my body that touches him is hot, and I despise myself for feeling the slightest thrill. Stupid social media propaganda.

Ruben glances at me. "I checked your file. You aren't married."

"Is that legal? To snoop around in employee files?"

"No," is all he says.

I don't have company files to research Ruben's life, but then again, I don't really need them. "Well, I checked Wikipedia, and you know what? It basically says you're a prat."

He chuckles, and we're so close together that I can feel his chest rumbling. If this keeps up, I may not need my coat. "You've read my Wikipedia page?"

"Pshhh." I lift one hand and wave it into the air. "I mean, I have, but I didn't really need to. I know more about you than any stupid site."

"And I thought I knew you. But maybe we both have secrets that can't be found in personnel files or websites."

My jaw flexes. "What do you want to know, Ruben?"

"Christian only said you came home with a baby. No one else came with you?" He's looking forward, pushing the stroller firmly.

"Christian doesn't know what he's talking about."

Ruben furrows his brows again. He's going to get some major frown lines. Then what will all his supermodel girlfriends think? "You didn't bring him from Vietnam? Or you two didn't come back alone?"

I've had two days to think about this. For as long as I'm able, I've decided to keep Moira's secret. I won't tell anyone that Axley is Moira's baby, but I also don't want to be seen as a big, fat liar when the news does finally break. So...I'll evade. Let people draw what conclusions they will, and at the end of the day, their conclusions will be their own problems, not mine. "No, I got him for Christmas."

Ruben's steps falter and he stops pushing. Immediately the stroller comes to a stop. I'd somehow been letting him do all the work. He glances down at Axley who rewards him by blowing a bubble with his lips. After a moment Ruben looks up at me. "Which Christmas?"

I just laugh. "Does it matter when or how I got him? I've got to take care of him, and I'm not taking him to Vietnam. We're staying here."

"And his father?" Ruben says this slowly, almost like he doesn't want me to ignore the question this time.

"Not in the picture." I could tell him he died—play the sympathy card—but the fewer people who know about Axley, the better. And since his dad really did die, it doesn't feel like something I should take advantage of.

His jaw clenches for a moment before he nods, as if a man leaving me alone with a child isn't surprising to him at all. "Then you'll need your position back."

It's my turn to be speechless. For a moment, anyway. I usually manage to find something to say. "You're giving me my job back out of pity?"

Ruben's jaw clenches and again, a deep line forms between his eyes. Yep, give him a few more years, and that smooth skin of his is going to be lined and…Crap—he's a man. It will just make him look distinguished. He'll be one of those men with peppered gray hair still leaving women breathless with his magnetism. Could life be any more unfair? "You are one of Palmers' best employees. Pity has nothing to do with it."

"And yet, you didn't offer me my job back until you met Axley."

His face freezes. He blinks twice before speaking. "You named your son Axley?"

Of all the things I'd just semi-told Ruben, this was the thing that surprised him most? "No, I just call him that for my health."

Deflection. I'm already getting better at it.

He shakes his head. "I'm sorry. That was extremely rude. Axley is a perfectly valid name. I just thought…"

What did he think? That he knew me well enough to know that I wouldn't name my child something ridiculous like Axley? Well, turns out he was wrong. Sort of. Anyway, I'm taking credit for surprising him even if it was Moira's doing.

We've reached the end of the block and I've no desire to extend the time I've spent outside freezing. I start to turn the stroller around and Ruben follows my lead. It slides around a bit, and I end up pressed against part of his back for the briefest of moments, but we manage the 180-degree turn.

Within three steps, our strides are back in sync. Ruben takes a deep breath. "So, will you take your job back?"

Now it's my turn to clench my jaw, and if it causes unbecoming lines on my face, so be it. There is nothing I want more than to throw his pity offer in his face and tell him I don't need a job at his stupid company. This man hurt me. He tossed me away in a way that his family never would have. For three generations our families have managed to remain close, despite the fact that his is now famous and intensely rich. But that generational friendship is ending with us. And I can't forgive him for that.

And yet, Christmas is coming, and we haven't bought anything for Axley yet. It's not like he'll remember that he didn't open nice presents on his first Christmas. But it might be my only Christmas with him, and I'm dying to spoil him a little.

Plus, there's Mom.

I might be able to get past my weird obsession with making it to the top of Palmer Hotels, but nothing would make Mom prouder than me working there again. "Fine."

"No need to be grateful."

"I'm not."

He smiles, and I'm reminded why this man is the face of the most luxurious hotel brand of the modern era. He's stunning. It's no coincidence that despite being a huge company before he hit puberty, what really made Palmer Hotels into the global power-house it is today was the world going crazy over this man. He nods and his dimples deepen. "I know."

I wish it was easier to hate him.

CHAPTER
EIGHT

Christian does a double take as he walks off the elevator and sees me at my desk. Then he smiles and strides over. "Got your job back, did you?"

"Apparently there was a mistake in the email system, and they didn't mean to fire me at all."

Christian raises an eyebrow, but I shrug as if to say that's the story and I'm sticking to it.

"A mistake in the system, huh?"

"Yeah. Weird, right?"

"Very weird."

"Someone told me you were the one to alert upper management." I lower my smile, not because I'm ungrateful, but because I *am* grateful and I want him to see that I'm not being flippant anymore. "Thank you."

He leans on my desk. "I'm just happy you're back."

"Me too."

Mr. Auger calls me into his office a few minutes later. He makes a hurried apology about the slip-up in the email system.

I shake my head. "You and I both know that wasn't what this was."

"Well, it was a slip-up somewhere, and if upper management

wants to call it an email slip-up, I'm not going to contradict them. Are you?"

I know what he means. This is exactly the type of situation a large company doesn't want to become involved in. I don't want the mess of a lawsuit either. "Definitely not. I'm simply happy to be back at work."

"And we're happy to have you back. You've done some really great things, and I was certain to point them out after I heard the news. Maybe that's why there was a change of heart."

"Maybe." I don't want to give Mr. Auger credit when Axley is the real reason I got my job back, but what does it hurt to let my boss feel good about himself? Standing up for me can be his good deed for the year.

The next few days fly by. Rebecca and I grab coffee almost every day and while it's not the same as when Emily was here, I'm finally starting to feel like I'm back to myself. Usually, our conversation centers around my time in Vietnam. Today is no different.

Rebecca chucks her coffee cup in the trash as we walk into the lobby. "What's your favorite thing you bought there? If I go for the hotel opening, what should I be on the lookout for?"

I tell her the name of my favorite tailor shop. "If you're there long enough, you should definitely order a few things. I may have gone overboard. Every time I got my order back, I was so impressed with the quality, I ordered something else. I might never have the chance to wear some of the things I bought, but I love seeing them in my closet."

"Okay. I'm definitely doing that."

"I'll email the name and location to you. It took me months to find the best place in Da Lat, but it was worth it."

I haven't seen Ruben all week. Which is fine. I wasn't expecting to. He felt bad about firing me when he found out I had a child to take care of, but that didn't mean he wanted to renew our friendship. Plus, he normally spends a lot of time in New York, in the secondary office, which houses more employees than the corporate office. Some executives don't want to live in a tiny town in Northwest Washington. Their loss. We step into the elevator and I scroll my phone for any emails I missed while we were out.

"Oh, my goodness," Rebecca blurts out. "I left something in my car. I'll see you up there."

What? We hadn't even been in her car. I glance up. She's already halfway out of the elevator and Ruben is striding towards it. Rebecca and I have only talked about Ruben a few times, but she had a major crush on him in college. Even married, she can't handle looking him in the eyes or interacting with him. In her mind, he's some uber famous celebrity who belongs on her wall, not in her workplace.

I have the strongest desire to join her. But both of us leaving would be too obvious, so I hold my ground and push the *hold door* button, despite the fact that the button just below it is much more tempting.

He steps in and glances at where my finger is. "You resisted the *close door* button, eh?"

I give a little laugh, as if pushing it rapid-fire and waving at him through the glass door all the way up to the fifth floor was the furthest thing from my mind. "I don't know what you mean."

"You definitely thought about it." He leans forward and presses the 15.

Show off.

I put a hand on my hip. Since the elevator is glass, everyone in the lobby can see us, and I guarantee Rebecca is watching us.

"Why would I do that?"

"Maybe you're scared of my animal magnetism?"

I snort. That doesn't deserve an answer.

The elevator grows darker when we hit the sixth floor and all we can see is the elevator shaft. Ruben steps toward the buttons and swipes a card over the controls. A beep sounds but the elevator keeps moving upwards.

"What are you doing?" My purse drops off my shoulder and onto the ground when I push him aside and try to figure out what his card did.

"I'm using my override card to prevent anyone from getting on the elevator."

"Will it prevent me from getting off?"

"For now, we aren't stopping on the 11th floor anymore."

I glance at the control pad and sure enough, my floor is no longer lit up.

"You can do that?"

He waves his card in the air. "Some of the executives would prefer not to chat with brown-nosers in the elevator."

"And yet you're okay riding with me?"

"You literally just snorted at me when I tried to make a joke. That's not how brown-nosing works."

"Yeah, but why are you holding me hostage? It can't be because you want to talk to me."

He raises an eyebrow. "Of course not. I simply enjoy taking all the pretty girls who refuse to acknowledge my magnetism on rides in the elevator." He loosens his tie and looks at me like I'm his next meal. "Animal. Magnetism." He says it slowly, and I want to laugh with him like I did when we were in high school. Because this side of Ruben is *so* fake.

Or...I could call his bluff.

What would that be like? For a split second I consider letting this one play out. But if Ruben's *Time Magazine* photo on the wall was inappropriate for the elevator, acting out the photo shoot would be far worse. Besides, I would be on the losing end of this joke the second I acted interested.

He takes a step toward me. Ruben's eyes land on my forehead. My bruise is finally gone. Is that why he's doing this? Did he take over the elevator to make sure I was okay?

Ruben pulls on his tie again and then raises an eyebrow like he's waiting for me to respond. I don't think I was supposed to notice that quick glance to my forehead. I wave my hand at him like I'm not affected. "Don't use your playboy charm on me. It won't work. Just because I have a baby doesn't mean I'm easy."

Ruben swipes his card again and hits the button for the sixth floor. We keep going up so I'm not sure what he's done. But the elevator stops a second later on floor 14, and without opening the doors, starts back down.

Where do I get one of those cards?

His eye catches mine, but only for a second before looking down at his hands. "Trust me." His voice is low and quiet, like he's worried someone on the other side of the door will hear us. "I've never once thought you were easy." When his eyes return to mine, he isn't faking some smoldering look or looking through me like I'm not there. His look is something else altogether. It's open and honest, and something deep inside me cracks. He hasn't looked at me like that for so long, I forgot he could. "I know exactly what you having a baby means."

Does he? His bold statement takes me out of the place where I'm trying to decipher that look in his eye. I'm still trying to figure out what having Axley means to me, and I'm pretty sure he wouldn't come close to guessing correctly.

I push myself off the wall near the panel. I'm not even sure when my back hit it. Probably when Ruben stepped closer. "What does it mean?"

He takes a deep breath, and this time his eyes don't glance away. "Someone finally got to you."

Got to me? What the heck does he mean by that? "You think I would let a man take advantage of me?"

His jaw clenches like he's ready to rush into battle over that comment. "No," he says through gritted teeth. He swipes the card again and pushes 15. "That's not at all what I meant. Geez, Cadence." He shakes his head like I said something horrendous, but he still hasn't answered my question.

"What did you mean, then?"

He rests his shoulder on the wall of the elevator. His deep navy suit is the kind that makes his arms and chest look like a marble statue women would rub their hands down for good luck. I have no idea how much a suit like that costs, but I'm guessing people don't typically lean against walls while wearing them.

He crosses his arms over his chest, accentuating the power of the suit. The briefest hint of a smile crosses his lips, but I barely catch it before it's gone. "You fell in love and you fell hard. You do everything one hundred and twelve percent, and as much as I've wanted to see that happen for you, I'm glad we were on different continents when it did." He pushes back off the wall. "Tell me I'm wrong."

I close my eyes for a second because he's way too close, and my immunity to Ruben Palmer might not be as potent when he's six inches from me in a confined space. He smells like those Christmas cinnamon pinecones I can't help but buy every year. They didn't have them in Vietnam, so lack of exposure must have made me especially vulnerable. The minute I get off work, I want to find some to take home with me. I open my eyes and I swear he's even closer. "You're wrong." My voice comes out quieter and shakier than it should have.

A wry smile spreads on Ruben's mouth and I can tell he thinks I'm lying. "I don't think less of you for falling in love."

His body sways toward me and I can't tell if he's going to hassle me for lying to my superior or...Holy Moses, is Ruben going to kiss me? Right here in the elevator? During company time? Like, would we be paid for kissing in the elevator? Technically, I guess we would, but how dishonest is that? I shouldn't get paid for kissing Ruben. I don't even want to kiss him, and I'm fairly certain he doesn't want to kiss me. His head dips lower and one arm is reaching down, to what? Grab my waist? My heart pumps faster and I'm breathing in his cinnamon scent like this is my last Christmas. I'm crazy. He can't be thinking of kissing me. Not only is it unethical and a completely inappropriate use of company time, but he has a freaking girlfriend. Daphne VanPelt, as in VanPelt handbags.

I stiffen at the thought of her name, and Ruben immediately steps to the side. He's still leaning down though, and he bends lower to pick up my purse. He hands it to me from two feet away with his arm outstretched. "You dropped this." I think I'm ready for the elevator to just snap its cables and send me crashing into the ground floor.

Of course, Ruben wasn't going to kiss me. And the second he saw the way my brain was working he couldn't get away fast enough. We ride in silence, passing floors 12 and 13. I guess we're done talking. He'll get off at 15 and then I'll ride down to my floor alone.

I'm not sure when I'll get another chance to speak to him and it feels like a loss. He'd always been the closest thing I had to a brother or a cousin, and it sucks that he ruined that. I risk a glance at him. His jaw is clenched, and he's looking at the crack between the doors, no doubt wishing that little magic card could make the elevator move to the 15th floor even faster.

I shouldn't be the one to extend an olive leaf, not when he was the one to do everything wrong, but I can't help it. "I've missed you." His head jerks toward me like maybe he misheard me. "Ever since the Redwoods project..." I pause, because I don't think pointing out all the ways he has hurt me is going to help the situation. I sigh, and just tell him the truth. "I hate that we never talk, and I'm tired of being angry at you."

His foot slides toward me and then goes back to where it had been. Like he wants to step closer but doesn't dare. "I can talk." He shakes his head like he's said something stupid, and I can't help but agree with him. Our problem has never had anything to do with capability. "I didn't think you missed me. I can...of course I can..." Ruben is stumbling on his words. I guess I hit a nerve. Finally, he forces a full sentence out of his mouth. "If that's what you want, I'll see what I can do."

And that, my friends, is what we in corporate America call a brush off. Need a permit from a city official in under a month? Need a contractor to hire and extra crew to meet deadlines? The answer is always what Ruben just said to me, and it always means the same thing—it's *never* going to happen. I try to calm the murder that must be in my eyes, but it doesn't really matter since he isn't looking at me. "Is it that hard to talk to me?"

That caught his attention. His head whips around and storms are brewing behind those mahogany eyes. "You know it is."

The elevator stops. We've reached the 15th floor. As high as we're going to go. He pulls his shoulders back and stands straight and it's almost like our conversation didn't happen. But just when I'm certain the doors are going to open and he's going to leave me here feeling totally lost, he swipes his card one more time, and this time he pushes the button for the 11th floor.

Neither of us say anything while the elevator descends. The few times I sneak a glance at him, he's wearing his Palmer Hotel's executive face, his back against the wall of the elevator. All business, but if he wasn't going to talk to me, why in heaven's name did he stay on the elevator? The door opens on the 11th floor, I stride forward matching his businesslike vibe and give him a short nod of farewell. He returns my nod without expression. I only make it three steps before turning around. "You know, Ruben, I don't think I'm that hard to talk to. You don't have to take me on a weird elevator ride to make it happen. You could just call or text. Heck, I'd even take an email."

His eyebrows lower like I've said the most confusing thing he's heard all week. More confusing than telling him I missed him. He pushes off the wall and looks like he's going to say something, but the doors close.

I sigh and wave to Sylvia. She smiles, but her eyes glance back at the elevator. I hate the fact that maybe she's proving me wrong and Ruben can't just call or text me when he wants. At least not if anyone in the office notices. Maybe friendship between a lowly employee and the future owner of all of Palmer Hotels is more of a puzzle than I thought.

Thirty minutes later I get an email from an address I don't recognize.

Cadence,

I know you've read online that I'm a prat, but I'd like to prove that's not true. Thank you for telling me that I could reach out to you. This is me, reaching out. I'd love to bring Axley a Christmas present, if you'll let me. I'm available on Christmas Eve, and I will come prepared to hold a normal conversation. Or at least as normal as I can be. Feel free to ignore this email if you feel like I'm overstepping any boundaries.

R.

My hands are frozen over the keyboard. Of course Ruben can come over on Christmas Eve. Ben, too, if he wanted to invite him. It's the day after tomorrow, but it isn't like I need to do anything special to prepare. If we're going to be in each other's lives again, he can deal with my barely decorated apartment.

"Is that a message from Axley's father? Is he in the States?"

I whip my chair around to find Christian reading over my shoulder. I mutter a curse, then flip back to my computer and turn off the screen. "Geez, Christian. You scared me."

"Sorry. I was wondering if you were done for the day and wanted to grab a drink. I acted a bit weird at your place, and I want you to know that Axley is cool, you know. I'd still be up for whatever."

Still up for whatever? Like, *despite* Axley? It's late in the day and I'm tired, and Christian is probably being kind, but his confession isn't helping him. "I'm finished. But I need to get home to Axley. I'll have to pass on drinks."

Christian nods and grabs my coat from where I left it sitting on the side of my desk. We walk to the elevator and I jolt when it pings open. There's Ruben. No word from him in almost a full week and then I'm riding in an elevator with him twice in one day. I don't move until I feel Christian put a hand on my lower back and usher me in.

"Good evening, Mr. Palmer," Christian says.

Ruben responds only with a nod, and even though I don't need help moving anymore, Christian's hand stays put.

We descend a few floors and Christian's hand is like fire on my back. Ruben is an executive and we're in the workplace. Why is Christian acting like he's staking a claim? I lean over to Christian so I can quietly tell him to move his hand, but before I get the chance, Ruben pushes the button for the fifth floor and the elevator stops.

I pause mid-whisper. Ruben takes two steps out of the elevator before turning around, looking hard at Christian's offending arm, and then looking up at me. "Did you get my email, Ms. Crane?"

There's that Ms. Crane again. "Yes."

"Was my proposal agreeable to you?" His tone is too icy to sound bored and businesslike.

I step to the side and Christian's hand finally drops. "Yes."

"I'll see you on Christmas Eve, then."

His eyes flash to Christian's for an instant, and then he's gone.

The door closes behind him and Christian immediately jumps away from me. "*He* is R? Ruben Palmer is the R from your email?" One of his hands covers his mouth. "Ruben Palmer is... When did you even..."

"Stop it, Christian. He's not."

"But he wrote that email."

I don't answer him. I'm more than done with Christian today. How dare he touch me possessively and read my email over my shoulder? "What is your deal today, Christian? Why are you acting so weird?"

"*I'm* acting weird?" His eyes widen and he gestures wildly to the floor above us. "I just found out Ruben Palmer is the father of your baby and you think *I'm* acting weird? No wonder you always turned me down."

I scoff. "I didn't *always* turn you down."

"*One time* you agreed to go out with me, but you didn't keep the date."

"And the only possible explanation is that Ruben is the father of my baby?" Who did Christian think he was? Actually Brad Pitt?

"It doesn't matter what I think." He swears softly. "Did he even know about Axley before you got back? You should have seen the way his face paled when I told him you had a child. I thought he felt bad about putting a single mom out of work, but…" He puts his hand to his forehead and opens his mouth to say something more when the elevator pings and three more people get on.

There are a few polite exchanges before the door closes and then we go down the last two floors in silence.

Christian follows me as far as the exit before I turn around and stop him with a hand to his chest. "I don't want you following me home."

"I wouldn't. I don't want Mr. Palmer thinking—"

"It has *nothing* to do with Mr. Palmer. I am done dealing with you today. I just want to go home, snuggle up with Axley, and watch some TV. If you breathe any of this to anyone, so help me, I'll make certain you're the next one on a plane to Vietnam."

Christian wrinkles his nose and looks as if he's about to say something, but I see the moment he changes his mind. I'm not just his coworker anymore. I might actually have the power to have him transferred.

I shake my head but resist the urge to roll my eyes. "Goodbye, Christian. I'll see you after Christmas." Maybe by then I'll have my dignity back.

CHAPTER
NINE

My apartment's been cleaned to within an inch of its life and I put up every holiday decoration I could find. Mom and I grabbed a few things last week from a drugstore to make the apartment more festive for Axley's first Christmas. The tree is a sad little thing that I thought was a steal of a deal until I had to put it together. Mom's tree goes together in three large pieces. This one came in fifty-two. To make matters worse, after Axley broke two bulbs near the bottom, I gave up on the tree looking like it came out of a catalog. The top half is covered in lights and bulbs, but the bottom half is bare.

The entire apartment shows evidence of Axley, but it's so much better than the sterile, empty structure it was just two weeks ago.

There's a knock at the door, and even if I hadn't known Ruben was coming over, I would have recognized it. His whole family uses the same knock. Three sharp raps, succinct and close together.

I pull open the door, expecting to see his face, but instead find his legs rocking what must be a pair of $600 jeans—and the bottom half of his torso. He's wearing a sweater that should disguise how good his abs look in paparazzi photos, but somehow doesn't.

The rest of him is covered in brightly wrapped Christmas boxes. I laugh and open the door wide. "I thought you said you were bringing Axley *a* present."

He peeks around the stack. "I couldn't bring one for him without bringing one for you and your mom. Is she here?"

I motion for him to come in. "Mom went home after dinner. She doesn't keep your celebrity hours."

Ruben ignores the celebrity comment, keeping his head to the side as his eyes give me a quick once over." Nice shirt."

Heat travels up my neck. My shirt is not nice. It's a baggy old sweatshirt with "Eve'n Christmas" splashed across a red and white Santa styled cowboy hat. I've worn it every Christmas Eve since Dad gave it to me the year before he passed away. It isn't as oversized as it was when I was twelve, but it's still loose. I cut the crew neck top out of it the moment after he gave it to me to be "cool," and it just never hung right after that. But it's tradition, and a way to remember Dad during the holidays. I'm not going to change that just because one measly famous person is joining the festivities.

He glances around my apartment. "Where should I put these?"

"Under the tree is typical." My hand is still on the doorknob. Something about having Ruben in my little apartment is unnerving. He doesn't seem to fit here. Everything about him is larger than life, and my apartment was only ever meant for me. It is purposely small.

But Ruben doesn't seem to notice how out of place he is. He kicks off his shoes like we're back in high school, and hanging out at each other's homes is the norm. Only this time it's just us. Not us and our families; not us and our friends.

He marches to the odd little tree and sets his presents down. There are at least six of them. I shake my head. "Did you bring something for my housekeeper and cook as well?"

He bolts upright and turns. "I didn't. Should I have?" His eyes are wide and he's no longer smiling.

I laugh. "No, Ruben. I don't have either of those. But you only told me you were bringing Axley a present. So I declare myself exempt from getting you one. I'm not going to feel guilty."

"I assure you, my only thought this evening is to bring your family presents and be as normal as possible." He crosses his hand over his heart like he's some sort of overgrown and delicious looking boy scout. "Making you feel guilty never crossed my mind."

That was an obvious load of crap. It totally crossed his mind. I can see it in the way the corner of his mouth turns up. He's enjoying the chance to one-up me. I grit my teeth together. If we are back on speaking terms, the normal he's talking about means one thing. Competition. "Leave your coat on, we're going out."

"Now?"

"Yes, now. Apparently I owe you a present."

"You don't owe me anything." He leaves his coat on, but sits down on my sofa. "And I like it here." He pats the seat next to him. "Where's Axley?"

"He's asleep."

"For the night?"

"No. He usually wakes up around 7:30, ready to go for a few more hours before he settles in for the night."

Ruben pats the seat again and I sigh. I can't exactly leave with Axley asleep, anyway. I sit and my sofa is suddenly transformed into what most of the female population would consider the most enviable place on earth. It dips down from Ruben's weight, making it impossible not to lean toward him. Our arms touch, but he's still wearing his coat, so he probably doesn't even notice. I lean against the back of the sofa so I don't completely fall into him.

He turns toward me. "You must be exhausted every morning."

I shrug. "I tried to adjust his bedtime routine last week, but if he goes to bed earlier, I don't get much time with him at all. This way, Mom spends the last little bit of her time with him while he naps so she gets a break, and I can decompress from work before he wakes up. After that, it's just me and Axley partying until about eleven."

Ruben kicks his legs out and rests them on my coffee table. A bit presumptuous of him. What if I didn't allow feet on my coffee table? But I do, so I prop my feet up too. Just to make him comfortable. It seems to work, since he sighs somewhere deep inside his chest and his head rolls back to rest on the top of the couch. "Sounds like heaven."

I snort.

He doesn't open his eyes, but I know he registered my unladylike chuckle, because the corner of his mouth turns up again. "No, it's true. I'm so tired of traveling all the time. Can't I just come here and hang out from seven-thirty to eleven every night?"

Is he serious? I was gone for three years and I never even got an email from him. He barely talked to me the two years before that, either. Him wanting to be here makes no sense. "Sure," I respond with a smile, because today is about talking, even if he is being ridiculous. This friendship or whatever we are trying to do will need the kinks worked out just like a brand-new hotel does. "I'll take your airplane and you watch Axley?" As I'm saying it, I'm not sure who would get the better deal. I'd freaked out finding Axley here, but our evenings together have become the highlight of my day.

He shakes his head. "Nope. You don't get my airplane. I just get to come here."

So he really does have an airplane. Of course he does. I remember when they put in the landing strip outside Ben's home. "What do I get, then?"

He turns his head toward me, his cheek resting on the back of the sofa. "Me?"

I snort again. This is becoming a problem. I swear I am not usually the snorting type. If the man hadn't practically fainted at the thought of renewing our acquaintance, I would think he was flirting. "If I get you, I get your plane, too." I cock my head to one side. "Oh my gosh, I'd get stock in Palmer Hotels. Mom would be so proud. I like this idea. I totally win."

He smiles, and it softens that bad boy charm of his. Or heightens it. I'm not sure which, but he definitely knows what he's doing. "You always do." He throws his arm on the back of the sofa. It isn't around my shoulders, exactly. Other than our thighs being pressed together due to the size of the couch, he isn't touching me. He's just resting his arm *above* my shoulders.

I should have made Christmas cookies, or apple cider or something. I'd practically challenged him to fix us, but nothing about this feels right. We were never alone when we were friends. I hated that he changed so much and made everything so distant and awkward between us, but sitting on my couch together with nothing to do just feels...off. If I were anyone else, I'd be tempted to put my head in the crook of his arm and make myself very comfortable on what was once described by vogue as *The World's Most Alluring Chest*. Seriously, those words were on the cover, and curse my currently overactive senses, because whoever wrote that title wasn't wrong.

It's been way too long since I've been alone with a man anywhere near my age. Ruben is so relaxed, he looks like he could fall asleep. I, on the other hand, am full of nervous energy. My toes tap against the coffee table. Neither of us talk, so at least I'm not saying anything stupid like, hey, I know we've only talked like six times in the last six years, but maybe we should make out.

I count to twenty in my head, because numbers are safer than the thoughts raging through my mind, and then I jump up.

"I really better get you a present."

He blinks up at me as if I just woke him from an afternoon nap. "It's Christmas Eve. Nothing is open."

"That's not true. The gas station is open."

He rubs a hand down his face and squints one eye in my direction. "You're going to get me a present from the Gas 'n Sip?"

I nod. "Would you prefer no gift?"

"Yes." He drops his head back down and closes his eyes again. "I already told you that. I was enjoying sitting here with you, and now you're going to make me go out into the snow again."

"You can stay here if you want. It shouldn't take me long."

He groans. "No way. I'm coming with you. You'll notice I didn't take my coat off."

I push my lips together. He's right. He's been egging me on, knowing it would drive me crazy if he one-upped me by getting me a present when I didn't get him anything. I try to be angry, but honestly, it's better that he thought that was what was driving me insane instead of thoughts of snuggling up with him.

"I'll get Axley. If he doesn't wake up soon, he won't go to sleep before Santa arrives, and I don't want him getting coal on his first Christmas."

My bedroom feels about a thousand degrees cooler than the rest of my apartment and I take a moment to breathe un-Rubenized air. What is wrong with me? I've read way too many articles about him. The Ruben propaganda is seeping into my brain. I creep over to my bed. Axley has been sleeping on it since the day he arrived. It's probably about time I buy him a crib. We've gotten everything else, but for some reason the crib feels permanent. Like, what am I going to do with it after he leaves? Moira must have a crib somewhere, unless she got rid of all his things before leaving the country.

I don't think I would have the heart to throw away his crib. I would become this weird single lady with no children who keeps a crib in her room. Like I'm not weird enough already.

Plus, I don't mind cuddling him back to sleep any time he wakes up. We both get more sleep that way. I don't care what the books say. I'm the temporary mama—I can spoil him a bit if I want to. I scoop him up and his arms reach above his head in a stretch. He makes a squawking sound that lands somewhere between kitten and creaky door. It's officially the cutest sound on the planet.

How could Moira have left him? No TV spot could be worth missing your son's first Christmas or the noises Axley makes. What if he outgrows them before she gets back?

I pull Axley close to me and carry him back to the living room.

Ruben is standing by the door, holding Axley's coat by the sleeves like a formal butler.

Or maybe a dad.

I'm going with butler.

I slip Axley into his coat which leaves him practically in Ruben's arms. I almost reach for him, but then stop. "Can you hold him for a second? I'm just going to grab him an applesauce for the road."

"Sure."

I pull my hands away and Ruben is left holding Axley far from his body, Axley's arms and legs dangling in the air. Ruben looks a little lost, but then turns Axley to face him and tucks him into the crook of his arm. Axley is only half awake, and despite the fact that he's only seen Ruben once, he snuggles into Ruben's coat.

Dang you, Axley. How'd you manage that so easily?

I turn away and dash into the kitchen, because being jealous of a toddler is dumb and thinking about Ruben Palmer like that is even dumber. I grab some food, only berating my fickle female heart twice, and then return. "Okay, I'll take him."

Ruben's cheeks are puffed out, making a face at Axley, and Axley is grabbing his nose. He looks up at me, lets the air escape slowly, and shrugs. "I don't mind carrying him. Are we taking the stroller or your car? I would offer to drive, but I don't have a minivan with a car seat yet."

Like so many other things, Ruben holding Axley feels wrong, like I shouldn't let Ruben get attached. It's bad enough that I've totally fallen for Axley. He'll always be my nephew, but who knows how often I'll see him after Moira returns?

I shake my head. "That's alright, I'll take him." Ruben's face falls, but he hands him to me. "You grab the stroller. The gas station isn't far, and I don't have a car yet."

Almost no one is out on the street this Christmas Eve, but at least this time the sidewalk has been shoveled. A light dusting of snow is lazily making its way down the horizon. It glistens in cones of light under each lamppost. We've stepped into the Rosco version of a snow globe. Maybe this whole freezing cold thing isn't so bad after all. Not if it gives me a Christmas Eve like this. Ruben's hands weave between mine on the stroller, even though I can totally manage to push it now that there aren't several inches of fresh snow on the walk. I let him. Making out on my sofa? Bad idea. Being pressed up against him while we push a stroller? Totally. We're a block away from the apartment when I realize I've been an idiot. Everyone in town knows who Ruben is, and he shouldn't be seen walking with me and Axley, especially not on Christmas Eve. I glance around, but no one's nearby.

"What's wrong?" Ruben asks.

"Someone's going to see us." I push him away from the stroller with my hip. "Stand a little farther away from me."

Ruben puts a hand to his heart and feigns hurt. "You don't want to be seen with me?" He frowns, then pulls his wool hat so low it covers half of his eyes, hunches his shoulders and twists his left foot, dragging it behind him. "Luckily," he says, his voice raspy, "I've got the perfect disguise. No one will think twice about us now, young lady. Your reputation is safe."

I think he's going for decrepit old man, but somehow he still manages to look more like a sexy pirate. The man can't look bad even when he's trying. I laugh and push him with my hip again. If anyone sets foot on this street, they will one thousand percent notice us. "Yes, *I* am the one that doesn't want my reputation tarnished." But then I freeze. Ruben straightens, immediately noticing my distress. Crap. "Actually, I don't want Axley to be seen with you."

He furrows his brows. "Are you worried about pictures of him? I know most of the people who take my pictures. We have a pretty good understanding in place. I'll make sure they know not to post anything about him."

"What do you mean, you know them?"

He shrugs. "I'm in a unique position. Most celebrities don't want to be in the tabloids, but I've been the face of Palmers for years, and every time there's an exciting news article about me, bookings at our resorts go up. So…"

"You tell them where you're going to be."

"Often enough that they don't have to follow me around when I'm in Rosco. Have you ever seen paparazzi here?"

Come to think of it, no. I glance at him sideways. A lamplight from across the street is directly behind him and the glitter of snow backlights his profile like he's in a moody photoshoot. Can't he ever look average, for once? He's basically glittering like Edward Cullen. "Let's say I believe this weird deal you have going on actually works. What about Mrs. Kramer? Or Geraldine Forrester?" I stop pushing the stroller and my eyes go wide. "What about your grandfather? We would never hear the end of it if he saw us like this together."

Ruben puts his hands back where they were on the stroller. "I think I can handle our old debate teacher and the town drunk."

A laugh burst from my throat and I hit him in the arm. "Mrs. Forrester is *not* a drunk."

"Why do you think she yells at people all the time?"

I push my lips to one side. He might have a point. "Okay then, what about Ben?"

He shakes his head. "Trust me, it wouldn't make my grandfather any worse than he already is. I thought perhaps with you in Vietnam he would give up on teasing me about you."

I laugh. "Only Ben can tease Ruben Palmer. Everyone else is too scared of you."

"He still treats me like I'm in high school."

"I liked you when you were in high school."

"No, you didn't."

"Sure I did. You weren't too big for your britches then."

Ruben's eyebrows furrow and he smirks. "I wasn't what?"

"Too big for your britches." I repeat, slower this time. He still doesn't seem to understand. "It's a saying. Surely you've heard Ben say it." This makes him smile, and I want to curse. I need to start hanging out with people my own age. "It means you think too much of yourself—like you've outgrown your pants." Ruben's eyes spark and he opens his mouth to say something, but then looks down at Axley and changes his mind. That dirty little perv. I groan. Why am I referencing his pants at all? "Please tell me you weren't going to say something gross, like that Daphne never complains about—"

He lifts one of his hands and covers my mouth. "Cadence, not in front of Axley."

I bite his finger—just a nip—enough for him to remove his hand. "So you *were* thinking that."

"Not exactly that."

I give him a victory smile. "Looks like I still know you pretty well."

"Not as well as you think."

"If that is some reference to your britches again…"

"Geez, no. Get your mind out of the gutter, Crane."

We cross the street in silence, and Ruben lifts the stroller over the curb. There are no cars filling up with gas or parked in the stalls, which means I'm the only person on this block still looking for last-minute gifts. Way to go, Cadence.

"Can I ask you a question?" Ruben asks.

I just bit his finger a minute ago. It's giving me whiplash trying to keep up with how this man goes from intimate to nearly professional in the blink of an eye. "Of course."

"Do you always think of me as Ruben Palmer?"

"What?"

"Just now, you said only my grandfather can tease Ruben Palmer. Is that how you think of me?"

I furrow my eyebrows and bend over to unbuckle Axley. "You *are* Ruben Palmer. How else would I think of you?" When I look up, he's looking at the two of us like he wants to say something but doesn't know how. It's a strange look on someone who's usually so self-assured. "Are you okay waiting out here? I can't really buy your present while you watch."

"You don't need—"

I cut him off. "Yes, I do. Deal with it. And no complaining about the quality either. There are only so many luxury items to be found at a gas station."

"Breath mints?"

"Dang it, Palmer." I use his last name just like our debate coach used to, and the furrows between his eyes soften. I'm not sure what's wrong with thinking of him as "Ruben Palmer," but I can think of plenty of other things to call him if that's what he wants. "Breath mints were on the top of my list. Now what am I going to get you? No more guessing."

He laughs and pulls Axley's beanie down lower so it covers his ears. "Okay, I'll wait here, and you better impress me. I got you something really good."

I raise an eyebrow at him. "You did?" What would be a really good present from someone with unlimited income? A Porsche? No, that's ridiculous. Where would Axley sit? Probably a Mercedes.

He narrows his eyes. "I see those wheels spinning. Fine, my gift isn't *that* good. Go get whatever you're getting. We both know you're only doing it to settle the score that only you are keeping."

He grabs both of my shoulders and physically turns me toward the gas station. The evening had started vibrant, but Ruben's last words ring a little hollow as I place Axley on my hip and amble forward. I'm the only one keeping score. He isn't. I'm the only one keeping tabs on the other. I don't have a massive social media following or news stories being published about me. Those things had allowed me to still feel a connection to Ruben after all these years, but if he'd wanted to keep up with me, well, he would have had to reach out. And he hadn't. Not even once in the three years I was in Vietnam. I'm not sure what brought him crashing into my world on Christmas Eve. When I'd said I wanted to talk again, I'd meant maybe we could chat at the water cooler, or have dinner with our families again, but this? This was new. Could it be because of Axley? If it is, I don't blame Ruben—Axley is pretty amazing. But it can't be just me. I've been accessible for years, and he's never even called to wish me a Merry Christmas before.

The door rings pleasantly when I push it open, and I force a smile at the little woman running the cash register. Poor thing. No one should have to work on Christmas Eve.

"Welcome," she says with a wave and a smile back. She seems perfectly okay being here. Maybe too okay.

I glance around the store. The first row of goods is all motor oil, work gloves, and funnels. My stupid brain conjures up a vision of Ruben in a photo shoot wearing jeans and no shirt, streaks of oil on his face and torso as he models the products I'm looking at. I switch Axley to my other hip and give myself a mental shake. What is wrong with me tonight? I'm looking for a present for Ruben, not endorsement deals that he would never take. Plus, if I had to hazard a guess, Ruben hasn't put oil in his own car...ever. I sigh. This is going to be an impossible task.

"Can I help you find something?" The woman's voice is strong for her age, and she's smiling like there's no place she would rather be on Christmas Eve. Axley squirms in my arms, but there's no way I'm setting him down on the floor of a gas station.

"I'm looking for a gift."

"For your little one?"

"No." I shake my head. "For the big one out there." I jerk my head toward Ruben.

The woman has to be pushing seventy with her spiky gray hair, but she still sizes Ruben up. Who wouldn't? Her name tag only says "MRS." in capital letters. She puts her hands on her hips and surveys the store like it's a problem to be solved. "Is he a drinker? We have some…well, I wouldn't say fine beverages in the back, but we have some beverages in the back."

Is Ruben a big drinker? I don't actually know. He must be, since he's always getting his picture taken at nightclubs. Although, I've never read an article that said he over-drinks. I don't know the over-twenty-one Ruben very well. "I don't think so. I mean, he could be, but I don't think so."

"We have a souvenir section. Maybe something from Rosco to remind him of his time here?"

I smile at her. We're more Rosco than almost anyone else living here. But mediocre alcohol and fossil fuel products are a no-go, so souvenirs it is.

Axley reaches for MRS. as we pass her and she touches his finger with a smile. The souvenir section has postcards with the lake, shot glasses that say The Original Palmer Hotel, and fridge magnets with both of those things. Holy crap. Am I really going to give Ruben Palmer a cheesy Palmer Hotels souvenir for Christmas? I grit my teeth. I hate being on the bad end of anything. He really should have warned me. No gift should ever be given without at least two days' notice. It should be a rule. And at Christmas time, it should be extended to four days to account for longer shipping.

Axley is leaning forward, trying to grab something off the shelf, and I cup his hand in mine to stop him. It's a mug that says in black and red lettering:

Only the NICEST people on the NAUGHTY list get to spend CHRISTMAS at THE PALMER HOTEL.

I cringe. But honestly, at least this might make him laugh. And he probably doesn't already have twenty of them. I grab the mug and bring it to the counter.

"Great choice." The little lady says. "Should I wrap it for you?"

Since when did a gas station have wrapping paper? Probably since this woman started working here. She scans the code on the sticker on the bottom of the cup and the scanner machine makes a beeping sound. MRS. looks up with her eyes sparkling. "Oh, I was hoping you would get this."

"Get what?"

"The prize." She looks at me like I should know what she means by that, then waves her hands and reaches under the desk.

If she pulls out a rifle, I'm chalking this up to being the weirdest night of my life. I shift Axley so he's partially behind me.

When she pops back up she's holding a red mini cannon, and not the dangerous kind. I relax as she pushes a button on the back and an explosion of canned snow bursts into the air. Axley jumps in my arms but then laughs as he tries to catch the snow in his hands. The lady laughs and claps her hands. "Your prize is a second matching mug and your choice of teas."

She runs to the back of the store and brings me back another mug, then pushes a box of individually sized tea packets forward. "Take two. Some are calming and will help you sleep, and others will give you energy."

I grab two of the calming ones. My brain really needs to calm down, and nothing sounds better than a solid night's sleep. She wraps up the present and I sneak a twenty into the tip jar. "Merry Christmas," I say when she hands me the bag.

"May your Christmas be filled with magic and surprises this year," she responds, and I can't help but smile. An elderly woman was the last type of person I would have expected to be working late on Christmas Eve, and yet, somehow she was the perfect person to be doing so. No one could leave this store feeling stressed.

When we get back to Ruben, he eyes the bag in my hand. "Did you find something good, then?"

I hold up the bag like it's a trophy. "I found something—that's for sure." I place the bag in his hand. It's the first present I've ever gotten him, and I'm pretty sure we both know it. Too bad it sucks. "Don't look inside."

I bend over to put Axley in the stroller. If you would have asked me a month ago what I thought I would be doing on Christmas Eve, never in a million years would I have guessed I'd be spending it with a baby and Ruben Palmer. And yet, somehow here we were.

Ruben's arm laces through mine again, and like an old married couple, we stroll lazily back to my apartment.

CHAPTER
TEN

Ruben entering my apartment for the second time isn't much different from the first time. He still seems like he stepped out of my TV instead of through my door..

I set Axley down and he toddles over to the Christmas tree, pulls on one of the cheap, individually-attached limbs, and plops down on his diaper-padded bum.

Ruben has his gift in his hand, and I'm tempted to send him on his way with it. He can open his tacky mug at his house, under his professionally decorated Christmas tree, and he and Ben can have a good laugh about how pathetic my present is. Ruben will toss the mug aside and shake his head. *And I gave Axley a Mercedes!*

Ruben pulls off his coat and drapes it over one of my kitchen chairs.

His sweater isn't hiding his arms very well. Come on, sweater, you have one job: to be bulky enough to hide the fact that scrawny Ruben Palmer hasn't been scrawny since he turned seventeen. The knots and braided weaves are all there, but somehow, they still manage to rise and fall with each curve of his arms.

I'm certain my ratty, cut-up sweatshirt is doing nothing for

Ruben. I won't ever win in a contest of not being distracted by the other. I'd rather win at speech. It just sucks that that victory was ten years ago. And I doubt he's feeling the effects today. I, on the other hand, need sunglasses that block out sweaters instead of the sun. Sweaterglasses.

Ruben slides off his shoes, strides over to the tree, and places the bag underneath it. I'm still just standing awkwardly in the doorway. The chance to convince him to leave has passed. "Make yourself at home," I say with just the slightest touch of sarcasm.

He smiles back so big that his stupid dimple shows. "I plan on it."

He grabs his stack of presents and sets them on the coffee table. I kick into overdrive, throwing off my coat and shoes in a split second. My sweatshirt slides off one shoulder but I ignore it. No way am I letting him sit on the sofa first. If he wants to sit next to me, fine. But it won't be my decision this time.

I plop down and pull my sweatshirt back up over my shoulder. A moment later he joins me.

My body dips toward him.

Or does he dip toward me? I check the slopes of our legs. Nope, I'm definitely the one dipping. Of course I am. We're sitting on a plush, sinking sofa and he weighs more than I do. It's science.

Ruben points at the stack of presents. "Should we start with the biggest one? It's for Axley."

"Axley gets the biggest gift?" I paste on a pout.

"Last time I checked, you were frustrated that I got you anything."

"That was before I got you something. Now that I'm prepared, I've got my hopes up. It's not every day that Ruben Palmer gets me a present." His full name slips out, because, well, it was the perfect chance to use it. Ruben bringing presents isn't such a crazy thought, but Ruben Palmer? I.N.S.A.N.E.

He doesn't flinch or anything, so I don't think I've hurt his feelings, but my brain finally catches up to what he meant outside the Gas n' Sip.

"I *could* bring a present every day, though, right? As long as I give you ample notice?"

"Four days at least. A week during the holidays," I answer, without skipping a beat.

"Alright, consider this your warning. Expect a present from me in one week."

What is up with Ruben tonight? I'm struggling to keep up. "A New Year's Eve present? Who does that?"

"Yes, a New Year's Eve present. I'm warning you, so order something off of Amazon asap."

He says "asap" as if it's a word, and for some reason, it takes me back to our debate days. It was just the type of thing that would have docked him points. He was always trying to be charming in an arena that didn't play by those rules.

Luckily for high school Cadence, I had no idea how to be charming.

I put my hand to my chest in mock horror. "As if I would order you something off of Amazon."

His eyes narrow. "You would definitely order me something off of Amazon."

"Fine. But it's not because I don't care. It's just so dang easy."

He shrugs in agreement. "And they have everything."

"Exactly. What if I want to get you one of those singing fish to mount on your wall? You think they have one of those at the Gas 'n Sip?"

"Probably not." He sits forward to scoot the gifts closer and his free hand lands on my knee. The gesture is so casual, he probably isn't even aware he's doing it. But my knee is aware. Very aware. "Unless that's what is in the bag. Because if the Gas 'n Sip had that, you'd better have bought it for me. I've always wanted one of those."

For some reason I believe him, and I know what I'm putting in my Amazon cart tonight. He's probably joking about getting me a present, but I'm not going to be caught unprepared again. "Sorry." I shrug my shoulders. "The closest thing to a singing fish was a tuna fish sandwich, and as much as I wanted to buy that for you, Axley stopped me."

Axley is pulling on branches and watching them pop back into place as he releases them. I stand up and Ruben's hand slides away. Immediately it's easier to breathe. I pick up Axley and bring him to the coffee table. I can't believe Moira is missing all of this. I pull my phone out of the side pocket of my leggings and snap a picture of him. I need to document Axley's first Christmas.

I have nowhere to send his pictures, but when she gets home, I'll share them with her. Ruben has the present in both hands and he smiles as he hands it to Axley. "Merry Christmas, Axley."

I hold up my phone and take another picture. "Look, Axley— a present." I pull a corner of the wrapping paper off to get him started.

"Here, let me." Ruben takes my phone and snaps a picture of the two of us. I smile and lean forward to help Axley figure this whole thing out.

The wrapping paper is that fancy thick stuff—the kind you could wrap a fish with, and no fish smell would escape. But then you would have a Christmas-wrapped fish, so that wouldn't really make sense. Unless it were a singing fish, but you could wrap a singing fish in anything.

I give the paper another tear, and the ripping noise finally gets Axley's attention. He looks up in avid interest. My phone makes a beeping sound. Ruben has decided to switch from taking pictures to recording. Axley grabs a corner of the loose paper in his chubby fist and pulls down. The wrapping paper makes a satisfying ripping sound and laughter gurgles out of his throat. I laugh and help him pull a little bit more. He doesn't seem to care at all what's under the paper, but as it rips under my fingers, our eyes meet and another laugh bursts out of him.

Christmas hasn't been this much fun in a long time, and it's not even Christmas yet.

I glance up at Ruben, and from the flash of contentment and the crinkle around his eyes, he must feel the same way. We smile at each other, and for a moment, the three of us could be the cover of a perfect holiday Christmas card.

Well, maybe not me, in my old leggings and even older sweatshirt, but Ruben and Axley one hundred percent could be. I step away from Axley and give Ruben the universal sign for stop recording by sliding a finger across my throat. He dutifully pushes the button and looks up from my phone, confused.

"Can you get some of him opening the present without me in it?" Ruben's eyebrows furrow, but he snaps a few pictures while Axley tears off a few more pieces of the paper, then hits the record button again. Moira might not want Axley to remember that she completely missed his first Christmas. She can have the pictures and videos of him opening presents without me in them, and I'll keep the rest.

Ruben stops recording. His dark eyes follow me as I sit back on the couch. "Are these for his dad?"

I glance up. His dad? The pieces of what he's been thinking fall into place and I want so badly to lie and say yes. That explanation would make the most sense. But I can't make my tongue lie to Ruben. Too much history. "No."

He snaps a few more pictures, his face blank, like he's purposely keeping it that way. "Will he be seeing Axley at all this Christmas?"

"No." This was getting weird. The last thing I want is for Ruben to think I'm a heartbroken, single mom. Although, bringing gifts and giving me my job back seem to be pointing to the fact that I am just that to him. "I'm going to start some tea." Axley and his present are forgotten momentarily and I practically dash the four steps into the kitchen to fill up my electric kettle and press the heat button. I gaze out the window to the street and take a few deep breaths. What am I doing? Axley is opening his first Christmas present, and I'm in the kitchen making tea? I close my eyes one last time, psyching myself up to look at Ruben again. He has no right to be so dang charismatic in my apartment. Smiles and glances like his belong on media feeds and magazine covers, not in here.

I turn around and focus on Axley. He has managed to get a big chunk of paper into his hand, but still doesn't seem to be all that intrigued by what's underneath the paper. But my traitorous eyes sneak over to Ruben's, and he isn't watching Axley at all. His eyes are penetrating and unwavering, and they're locked on me.

"If he were my son," Ruben's head tips toward Axley. "I would want to see pictures, at least."

I swallow. Ruben Palmer is a playboy, a world traveler, and a man impossible to hold down. I don't know if it's because I know his parents and love his grandfather, but at this moment, he isn't *that* Ruben. That Ruben is only a caricature of the complex man in front of me. "If he were your son, you'd be in the pictures."

Ruben's jaw clenches, and a cloud passes over his eyes. He leans forward as if he's about to respond, but instead he narrows his eyes and turns to Axley. The big chunk of wrapping paper in his hand is wet and starting to come apart in pieces. He brings it to his mouth, and Ruben pulls the soggiest bits off of his hand. I don't dare look at Ruben's face, but the one hand I can see is clenched at his side.

He is angry.

Angry that Axley's dad isn't here, and that I don't plan on sending him pictures. Neither of those reasons are justified. For all I know, Axley's dad would have gotten clean for him, just like Moira did. Maybe that's how he ended up overdosing. Perhaps he slipped up and his body couldn't handle the drugs any more. I chance a look at Ruben. He's staring forward, no longer looking at Axley, his jaw still clenched tight. I forget the tea, walk back to the couch, and place a hand on his arm. The ecru colored sweater is exactly as soft as I thought it would be. "I can't send those pictures to his dad."

Ruben faces me, waiting.

I take a deep breath and sit down next to him. He won't be angry anymore once I tell him the truth, but I really don't want his pity. For Axley, sure, but I hate that he's going to feel sorry for me. "He died before Axley was born."

CHAPTER
ELEVEN

uben's face goes slack and it takes him a moment to process what I said. "Oh, Cadence." His voice is so soft and low I barely hear him. "I'm so sorry."

I shake my head. "You don't need to be sorry for me. Just Axley."

Ruben swallows and glances at Axley again. One whole side of the present is visible. It's a box with a swanky wood car garage—the kind that cost triple what a plastic one would. This isn't something he picked up at the store yesterday. Nothing in Rosco carries anything quite so upscale. Not unless the hotel put a toy section into the gift shop while I was out of the country.

His lips purse together. "I should have gotten him something better."

I shake my head and pinch the soft knitted fabric between my fingers. "You didn't need to get him anything."

"I know I didn't need to, but I wanted to, and I should have gotten him something better."

"He's going to love it. He doesn't have enough toys."

"You must have had to leave a lot behind in Vietnam."

I want to nod but that feels dishonest. So I don't say anything. Instead, I jump off the couch, pull the last of the soggy, crumpled wrapping paper out of Axley's hand, and help him get the rest of the wrapping paper off in one big chunk.

"Cars!" I say to Axley in an overbright voice that matches only his mood. "Let's open the box."

The garage is made up of a few pieces that need to be assembled. Ruben and I sit on the floor so we can do it together. He grabs the instructions, which have exactly zero words on them, and flips to the first page. After studying it for a moment, he hands me the largest of the wooden parts. I grab it from him, and his fingertips slide softly over the knuckles of my hand. The gesture isn't accidental.

He's worried about me.

There are only seven pieces in total, and each time we stack one part on top of the next, I wait for that brush of our hands. Every time the contact lasts a little bit longer. And each moment is a repeat of his words earlier. *I'm so sorry.*

When the last piece clicks into place, I'm nearly in tears over a man I've never met. I blink my eyes fiercely and stand up. Six cars of different shapes sit at the bottom of the box, and I hand one to Axley. Ruben takes out another and places it at the top of the garage. Axley follows suit. Then Ruben places his large, tanned hand over Axley's chubby baby-pale one and gives the car a push. It rolls down the ramp and Axley bounces up and down in delight. Ruben hands him another car, and Axley pushes it hard enough to fall off the ramp.

Eventually Axley's excitement calms down enough that he can push the cars down on his own, and he does so repeatedly. We play with him for a while before Ruben stands up next to me. His little finger grazes mine, and when I don't pull away, he takes my hand and leads me back to the sofa.

I've known Ruben for over twenty years and he has never held my hand. I can't even remember us touching at all, before this week. Which is strange, right? In all of our interactions, surely we had to have hugged or something. But if we did, I don't remember it.

His actions are borne of pity, but his hand feels oddly at home in mine, as if we should've been holding hands for years. As if we've wasted a lot of time *not* holding hands. We sit and I don't stop myself from sinking into his side. Our hands land on his leg and I wait for him to drop my fingers but he doesn't.

I want to squeeze my fingers together, just to assure myself that this isn't some strange dream. But I'm pretty sure most dreams involving the man sitting next to me would be escalating to something more by now. We're sitting on a couch playing the world's most unengaging—but also, somehow, the most tantalizing—game of chicken. Who will let go first?

Not me and my Ruben-fantasizing fingers. How many times have I typed his name into a search engine? Could I really blame them for wanting to inspect him personally? I've been unknowingly training them for this since the day he became the poster child of every teenage dream.

I don't have an excuse for Ruben's fingers though, and every once in a while his thumb glides over my knuckles as if he's checking to make certain they're still there. Why? Surely nothing about my knuckles can be more interesting than those of the supermodels and social media darlings he typically dates.

I don't date anyone. So my curiosity is totally justified.

"We should probably open our presents." I say, because I can't keep my dumb mouth shut.

Ruben nods but he makes no move to stand up and get them.

What if I want to change my mind about the present I got him? What if instead of a mug, I scoot onto his lap and kiss his brains out? If he would take make-out sessions in exchange for gifts, I wouldn't need a week's notice. He could bring me presents any day of the week.

My hand does tighten then, because somehow I've let one thought conveniently stay out of my mind. Ruben has a girlfriend. A famous, hot one, and he's holding my hand because he feels bad for me as a single mom, not because he wants my tongue down his throat.

Not that I would put my tongue down his throat. I'm a much better kisser than that. At least, I think I am. It's been a very long time, and Ruben has way more experience than I do.

That thought, more than anything, is what gives me the fortitude to let go of his hand and pick up his present from under the tree and add it to his pile on the coffee table.

He doesn't complain when I leave him, but I do hear the soft thud of his hand landing empty on his leg. When I return with his brown paper bag, Ruben leans forward and grabs a thin rectangular gift from the table. He smiles, and most of the sadness of the last few moments has left his eyes. "Open yours first."

I narrow my eyes at the present. So mine isn't the pretty little box that looks like it could be jewelry. Noted.

I smile back, because I'm so done being sad on Christmas Eve, even if the handholding was worth it. Also, now that I have a gift for him, no way am I feeling guilty about getting one from him. The last two Christmases I opened a few gifts I bought myself while on Zoom with Mom, and it's high time I ripped open wrapping paper without knowing what was hiding underneath it.

I set the other gifts down on one side of the coffee table and I sit on the other. Because maybe I shouldn't sit next to Ruben in that droopy couch anymore.. I'm close enough to the couch that our legs intertwine, just as our hands do when we push the stroller. My leg, Ruben's leg, my leg, Ruben's leg. We're like a fancy layered sandwich. So yeah, my brilliant plan of making distance between us pretty much backfired. But hey, at least now we aren't touching. Not unless one of us moves more than an inch. I hold my hand out and he places the gift in it. My excitement must have shown, because suddenly Ruben is grinning with that soft gaze of his.

I scowl in return. "Don't give me your *Teen Heartthrob* smile. I positively can't handle it. Save it for the paparazzi."

"My what?" His smile fades into a more manageable lopsided grin.

"You know what I mean. That smile. The one that put you on the map and on every teenager's wall when we were in high school."

His smile falters a bit. Is he being self-conscious? He used to blush all the time when people mentioned it, but he had to be over it by now. That smile had made his company millions of dollars. Maybe more than millions.

"That's just how I smile."

"No, it isn't. You're purposely making your eyes do that dreamy thing. You know it gets you whatever you want."

He tips his head to one side. "Whatever I want, meaning, for you to open your present?"

I laugh. "I guess. But you didn't need to use your powers on me. I was going to open it anyway. It has been way too long since I opened a present I didn't buy for myself. Getting packages to Vietnam was…tricky, so I told Mom not to bother."

Ruben's eyes slide to Axley again, and I bite my lip. I need to be more careful. If I really had fallen madly in love and had a child while in Vietnam, I didn't want Ruben to think it was with some chump who didn't even buy me anything.

I grab the present out of his hand and feel it. I've read enough books in my lifetime to know that's what I'm holding. It's a hardback of middling length. What kind of book would Ruben choose for me?

Hopefully one with at least a side plot of romance. I tear open the book to find a plain, black cloth-covered book with gold lettering. *Dictionary of Difficult Words.*

I look up in surprise. "You got me a dictionary?"

He raises an eyebrow. "Not just any dictionary. A dictionary of difficult words. I saw it in a bookstore and thought of you."

"What bookstore?" I turn the book over in my hand. I don't think it's a recent edition. This is the kind of book you might find in a high-end shop, or maybe one that specializes in antique books. Rosco doesn't even have a bookstore, and I'm certain he hasn't left Rosco since yesterday.

His smile falters a bit, and then he waves his answer away. "It doesn't matter. I got it for you because you like to be such a smart a—." He breaks off the last word with a sidelong glance at Axley "Aleck."

I smirk. "I really do like being a smart aleck."

"I know."

And the weird thing is, I love this present. I don't even care that Ruben is doing his *Teen Heartthrob* smile on me again, because I'm flipping through the pages of the book and catching sight of some seriously obscure words. "Looks like this calls for a test of your vocabulary, Mr. Palmer."

I'm supposed to call him by his first name, but at least Mr. Palmer is different from Ruben Palmer, and he doesn't seem to mind. He does, however, shake his head. "No, I assure you, it does not. We both know you're much smarter than I am, and we don't need to prove it."

"That, my dear Ruben…" I throw his name out and his eyes flash. One side of his mouth quirks up. A strange lightness fills my chest. What in Mount St. Helen's am I going to do with that? For now? Ignore it. "Is where you're wrong." I flip the book open to a random page and, while keeping my eyes on him, run my finger down the page and stop in the middle. I look down. "Finifugal," I say and cock an eyebrow at him.

Ruben runs a hand down his face. "I think I'd rather play cars with Axley."

"Come on, give me a guess."

He groans. "A…" He pauses and scrunches one eye closed. "…good-hearted lord, way back during times when knights lived."

I press my lips together. "Nope."

We're silent for a moment. I wait patiently until his head lifts. "What? You want me to guess again?"

I lift one shoulder and my sweatshirt falls off of it. His eyes follow the movement and I stop breathing. I swallow hard and pull up my shirt. "Only until you get it."

He shakes his head and leans forward and before I understand his intention, grabs the book out of my hand. I try to wrench it back, my left hand a vice grip on his forearm while my right thrashes in the air. Our legs become even more entangled because both of us are most definitely moving more than an inch. He holds the book higher. I could reach it if I stood, but then he would just do the same and I like how we're sitting. I drop my hands in defeat.

He warily brings the book down to his eye level, all the time watching me. He makes a big deal of scanning down the page until he finds the word. "Finifugal, adjective. Of or pertaining to shunning the end (of anything)." He closes the book and looks at me over the dark black edges. "I was close."

"You weren't close. I think you mixed up fugal and feudal."

"I may have been thinking feudal, but I wouldn't say I mixed them up. You made me guess a word that I'd never heard before. I said the very first thing that came to mind."

"Lords and knights."

"Yes, I'm always thinking of those things. That smile you like to talk about? I think my face looks like that when I am pondering what a knight wears under that thick, clunky armor."

"I'm not sure they wear anything under there."

"I'm pretty sure you're right."

"So you're telling me that when you make that gorgeous face, you're dreaming about knights' underwear?"

His face is the epitome of seriousness. "That's what I'm telling you."

I shrug, trying so hard to keep down a laugh that's bubbling just under the surface. "Well, at least it isn't anything embarrassing."

He chuckles, which means either I've won the don't-laugh-at-each-other's-funny-jokes competition or he isn't aware that we're competing. "Exactly."

"Well . . ." I want to say 'my dear Ruben' again, but my heart is already acting too weird. "If that really is what you're thinking about when your face gets that dreamy look, I'm surprised I haven't heard of it before. That is a long time to be obsessed with knights."

"The longest." He opens the book without looking away from me and does the same trick I did. After his finger comes to a rest, he looks down. "Chandelle."

"Is it CH-andelle, or SH-andelle?"

"Does it matter?"

"Of course it matters. How am I supposed to guess the word if you aren't even pronouncing it correctly?"

"You aren't supposed to guess." He smiles. "You're supposed to admit defeat."

"I can't admit defeat when you already missed your word. At the very worst it's a tie."

He leans forward and suddenly our faces are only inches apart. "It is chandelle. With a ch. And I'm not giving you any more clues. No wonder you were better than me in debate."

I smile slowly and deliberately. "Thank you for bringing that up." He probably doesn't think about it nearly as often as I do, but at least he thinks about it.

"No more stalling. I need a definition."

Chandelle. It sounds a bit like a chandelier, but I can't really guess something like that after teasing Ruben for trying to combine fugal and feudal. The only word I can think of that ends in "elle" is organelle, which I've always thought of as a "small" organ inside of a cell. All I can think of for the "chand" part of the word is a chandelier. Crap. I have no idea. But I can't let him know that.

"I don't need to stall. Unlike you, I know the definition of my word."

He raises an eyebrow but doesn't say anything.

Here goes nothing. I tip up my chin. "It's a small lamp. Something you might set on a table or even hang somewhere in the house."

He looks down at the book and narrows one eye. Did I get it or not? I can't tell at all by his expression, and he isn't saying anything.

"Well?"

He pushes his lips together. "What kind of lamp, exactly?"

I ignore the fierce need to pump my fist in the air. I was right. Or at least very close. I just need to keep bluffing and he'll admit it. "A small one, you know, not like a big hulking one you put on the floor or anything." I need to be less specific, since he's obviously trying to trap me into saying something incorrect. "It gives off light—helps people see in the dark. That kind of thing."

"And where did you learn this word?"

"That's not part of the game. Probably from reading. I can't remember exactly. Do you remember where you learned all the words you know?"

His head cocks to one side and a slow grin spreads on his broad mouth. "I remember learning the word finifugal."

The slightest of laughs sneaks out at that, but I'm almost certain he isn't competing the same way I am, so I let it slide. "That's because you learned it today. Chandelle is just stuck somewhere in my memory, waiting to be used when the time is right."

"Now's your time, baby. Use it," he demands, crossing his hands over his chest. The timbre of his voice is suddenly deep and sexy. This isn't a *Teen Heartthrob* voice to go with his *Teen Heartthrob* smile. It's a grown-up voice that has me thinking some of my least favorite thoughts. Ruben, alone with one of his girlfriends, using that exact sonorous tone.

And what's with the *baby*? That is not helping my imagination. Or it is helping it, just in unnerving and distracting ways.

I squeeze my eyes closed and take a deep breath. "Despite the daylight coming in from the kitchen window," I open my eyes and nod to the large window directly in front of us. He uncrosses his arms and opens the book to follow along. "In the evenings, this room could use a few chandelles to brighten the corners."

He heaves a deep and disappointed sigh, nods in defeat and snaps the book closed.

I totally fist pump. And he smiles like he's been waiting for it, but I don't care, I've still got it. I can bluff my way out of—. Wait.

The book didn't snap. When he closed it, the book didn't snap. His finger is still marking the place where he found his word and a sick little worry makes the corner of my mouth fall.

Crap.

I've just been had. And there's nothing I can do about it. I've already celebrated my superior difficult-word knowledge. I've crafted a ridiculous sentence with a word I know nothing about. The only question that remains is how he's going to make me pay for it. His thumb is slowly making its way to the bottom pages as if he's going to flip the book open again and tout the real definition at any moment.

"Axley," I say brightly. "Do you know what kind of car that is?" Axley looks up, but I don't think he's registered my question. His hand is wrapped around a chunky wooden car that can't possibly be patterned after a real model. "It's a blue one."

Colors. I should be working on colors with Axley. My comment to him makes complete sense, actually. I grab another car off the table and hold it up. "This one's red." I pop up and march into the kitchen. "I'm going to grab you some dinner."

I hear a sigh behind me, and if I'm not mistaken, the sound of my present being closed completely. For the moment, I am spared the mortification of being told I was wrong. Not that I can't handle being wrong now and again. Just not where the Palmer family is concerned, and that goes double for Ruben. I've got issues, apparently, but I'll deal with them later. From the corner of my eye I see Ruben join Axley on the floor. He rolls a car off the top of the ramp and it crashes into Axley's foot. Axley's eyes go wide as he laughs and grabs it. If I were living in a movie, the camera would zoom in on the two of them, and the audience would sigh.

I reheat a plate of Mom's shepherd's pie, put Axley in his high chair and hand him a spoon even though I know he's just going to eat with his hands. Both Mom and the parenting books agree it's good for him to try to use one anyway.

Ruben is back on the sofa and Axley is eating just fine on his own. I sit back down on the coffee table and grab the bag containing Ruben's present. "Your turn," I say brightly.

Something is warring behind Ruben's eyes. He sneaks a peek at my dictionary, but then his eyes dart back to my gas station treasure. He *has* to want to tell me I'm wrong. But he also seems curious about my present. He scoots forward and his knee bumps my thigh. I suck in a sharp breath and immediately force my body out of high alert and into neutral. Why is my body so aware of him? I glance at Ruben and today is my lucky day, because he's reaching for his present, and I think he missed my propaganda-induced chemical response to him. His thumb grazes my fingers, and instead of pulling his present away from me, he pauses. I'm channeling a jellyfish floating in the ocean. I have no nervous system. I don't even feel how warm and intoxicating that digit of his is. He has a girlfriend, right? When was the last time I saw him and Daphne in the media? More than a week. Maybe two weeks.

I wait for him to pull the bag to him, but he doesn't. He's just as frozen as I am. Then, instead of taking the bag, his fingers tighten over mine and he leans to the side, bringing his mouth next to my cheek.

Breathing suddenly becomes dangerous. Ruben is so close, I could turn my head and kiss him. Does he want me to? Is this what he expects to happen anytime he makes it into a woman's apartment? It can't be. It isn't like I'm one of his...his...my vision goes a bit hazy. Ruben's free hand tucks some of my hair behind my ear and I should definitely, maybe, turn my head for a kiss.

But I can't do it. Twenty-eight years of knowing Ruben and

not kissing him has made it nearly impossible to change that statistic. But the decision might not be up to me, because Ruben is slowly lowering his mouth toward my ear. His breath is on my neck. "Cadence…" His voice rolls over me, low and deep and even better than his cologne voice. I want to start a protest on the street—a march demanding Ruben use this voice more. I should be able to listen to it online anytime I want. "Chandelle: a steep, climbing turn executed in an aircraft to gain height while changing the direction of flight."

I close my eyes. Freaking Ruben. Of course. Of course this is what he's doing. Proving me wrong *and* relishing in the fact that he can pretty much turn any woman into a puddle. The next time I get a free moment alone, I'm going to scan that book until I find a difficult word that means odious, and I'm going to use it on him.

I scrunch my nose and open my eyes. He pulls his present out of my hand and sits back as if he hadn't just made my breath hitch. We both missed our difficult word definitions, but he won the game. Without a doubt. His smile is different—innocent and guileless, as if he's never done one wrong thing in his life.

And he probably hasn't.

I refuse to go down this way. "I suppose some people might like to use the word that way."

He raises his thick, model-worthy eyebrows. "Probably airplane pilots."

I press my lips in a hard line, but I can't hold it. The corners of my mouth lift. I tip my head to one side. "Who's the smart aleck now?" I resist the urge to stick my tongue out at him, even though that would absolutely make him laugh. "Just open your gas station Christmas present, already."

His innocent smile is replaced by an honest-to-goodness grin, and he makes short work of taking the present out of the bag and tearing off the wrapping paper. Ruben turns the mug so he can read it. His eyes glance at me over his present and something flashes in them. "I love it."

Based on that flash in his eye, I might actually believe him, which is dumb, right? Why would he love a cheesy mug that has his own hotel's name on it?

"It was either that or motor oil."

"As much as I love motor oil, I think you made the right choice."

His dimple is showing, but there's no way I'm going to fall for his heartthrob smile twice in one night. I jump up from the table and grab his mug from him. The water finished boiling ages ago. "I got a matching one." Based on the way his smile deepens, he likes that too. "I'll make tea."

I dash over to the kitchen, wipe Axley's mouth even though it will be a mess again in 2.5 seconds, and take my time pouring the hot water into our mugs. I rip open the first of the tea bags and drop it into Ruben's cup. It isn't until I'm tearing open my bag that I notice the writing on it.

"Chamomile Xtra: Xtreme Calm." Well, I'm in need of some xtreme calm. I debate taking both of them for myself and giving Ruben something else, but his is already in the mug, so hopefully one bag will make my stupid heart settle.

"Sugar?" I call out.

"Yes?" His answer is a question, but I pretend I didn't notice the inflection in his voice as I dump a teaspoon of sugar into his mug. I do the same for mine, take a deep breath and one fortifying gulp of my calming tea, and walk back to the couch.

I hand Ruben his mug and he smiles at it again, like he's received the best gift in the world, instead of a gas station trinket.

Axley has resorted to throwing his food now. That's his way of telling me he's done. I wipe Axley and the floor down and then bring him back with me to the sofa. I sit, pressing my side against the arm of the sofa in hopes that my thigh will not have to touch Ruben's, but my plan doesn't quite work. Whose idea was it for me to only get one tiny sofa? Once the holidays are over, the first thing I'm going to buy is a big sectional with plenty of room for a crowd.

Axley smells like mashed potatoes, but thanks to his industrial bib, his clothes stayed mostly clean. This whole evening feels like I'm living in an alternate reality where Ruben was just a kid from my high school and not the face of Palmer Hotels. It's almost like the past five years of silence never happened. Like we lost touch a little during the college years, and when I came back to work for his company, the Redwoods project never happened. We kept meeting for coffee here and there, chatting in hallways when we saw each other and exchanging memes. Ruben never got tired of me or defensive about my ideas and we were just…us.

And in this dream reality, this Christmas Eve feels like a turning point—an evening where we both realize we want to share more than just memes with each other.

Axley yawns. Perhaps I should use that as an excuse to send Ruben packing, but he hasn't finished his tea yet, and I still have at least three tablespoons of liquid sitting in my mug. I pull Axley to my chest and reach for my tea. Ruben sees what I'm trying to do and hands it to me.

I take a few slow sips but I'm careful not to finish it. Ruben glances up at the clock. It's only 10:45 but it feels much later. "You watch TV with Axley until 11, right?"

I nod.

Ruben grabs the remote and turns on the TV. He flips channels until he finds a cheesy Christmas movie and stops. It's exactly what I would have chosen if it was just me and Axley tonight.

A few minutes later, the edges of the room are starting to get hazy. If I hadn't fixed the drink myself, I might have thought Ruben had put something in it. Not that he ever would. I blink my eyes. Why are they so heavy? The combination of Axley falling asleep on my chest, whatever that xtreme ingredient is, and about two weeks of bad sleep is all catching up to me.

I shift so I can lean back, away from Ruben, but that makes my legs push up against his. I'm past caring, and this way Axley can snuggle deeper into my chest.

I close my eyes, just for a moment.

A warm weight settles over my shoulders. Ruben's arm. It's heavy and warm, and much more comfortable behind my head than it has any right to be.

"Come here." His voice is low and he pulls me closer to him so that my head ends up on his shoulder and my legs shift the other direction. I guess that's a win, right? My legs aren't resting against him anymore, but my head is, and it feels divine. I'm going to let my foggy brain live in my little dream world a bit longer. Daphne doesn't exist here, and Ruben and I are such good life-long friends, resting my exhausted head on him just makes sense.

There's a shift beside me and I crack open an eye to see Ruben kicking his legs up onto the coffee table. I take the opportunity to shift lower, so my head is on his chest instead of his shoulder.

That was smooth, right? He probably didn't even notice. He smells amazing. His warm solid chest feels like coming home for Christmas.

Axley decides to stretch out over both of us. His head is still on my chest, but his legs are now resting on Ruben. I don't blame him. Not one bit. "Is this okay?" I mumble, because suddenly this man's only exit is blocked not only by me, but by twenty pounds of cuteness.

His head dips low into my hair, and he nods against it. "Yes. Everything about today has been more than okay." He inhales, and I wish I smelled like cinnamon. "It's been finifugal."

I'm sure he used that word wrong, but I'll deal with that sometime when I'm not cozied up next to him. I smile and settle in deeper.

I'm pretty sure I'm already asleep when Ruben's other arm lifts up to cradle both me and Axley. "He's a good kid." His voice is gravelly, like he hasn't used it for a while. Maybe he hasn't. I have no clue how long I dozed off. "I'm sorry about his dad, but I'm not sorry you're back in Rosco."

I stretch just enough to find an even more comfortable spot against him. "It's good to be home."

His grip tightens on me and I can't help but feel like Rosco wouldn't be home if Ruben wasn't in it. Which is ludicrous. It's my home because I grew up here and Mom is here.

Ruben takes a deep breath and my head rises and falls with his movement. "You loved him, right? Enough to settle down?"

Even with my foggy, sleep-deprived brain, I know who he's talking about. Axley's dad. I match my breathing to Ruben's and wait for two breaths before I answer. "I didn't really know him," is all I can manage before I fall asleep.

CHAPTER
TWELVE

My shoulder is stiff, but my head is supremely comfortable. Like, I'm-never-moving-from-this-spot comfortable. A noise woke me up, but it's hard to care what it was. I shift my shoulder so it falls deeper into the space between Ruben's chest and arm, when a loud banging on my door makes me wince.

I blink my eyes open. Light is streaming in from the window across from us, and for a moment I can't understand it. Did we sleep here all night?

My warm human pillow shifts underneath me. "Merry Christmas." Ruben's voice is throaty and muffled by my hair. I squeeze my eyes closed again. I'm not quite equipped to deal with the fact that Ruben, Axley, and I all slept on my sad excuse for a sofa. If my shoulder is sore, his back, neck, and pride must be even worse off.

But I have to face him at some point, so I lift my head, and with a grimace, manage to croak out, "Merry Christmas back." It seems like the point in the fairy tale or fever dream where one of us should bolt away from the other, but instead, neither of us moves. He doesn't pull me in closer, which would mean...well... something, but he also doesn't bolt up and say, *What the crap,*

Cadence? I slept here? Do you know how many places I need to be? We're stuck somewhere between those two scenarios, and it's a scary place to be.

I should bolt, right?

Knock, knock, knock. This time it's even louder and more urgent.

Ruben smiles down at me, and the combination of that smile, his deliciously disheveled hair, and the fact that I am literally curled up into him releases some sort of primitive reaction. Ruben is the forbidden fruit. He always has been. But I'm suddenly Team Eve, thinking one little bite couldn't hurt. He tips his head to one side, and my fingers tighten around his sweater. If he could hear my thoughts, I'd be a dead woman.

"It sounds like someone needs to talk to you."

I cannot move. My arms, legs and torso refuse to relinquish the warmth of his body. I let my eyes flutter closed. "I'm still sleepy." Sleepy. That is a completely rational reason to stay where I am. It has nothing to do with the fact that I'm fairly certain I'm living in a dream that won't repeat itself. "It can wait."

The pounding starts again. Ruben clears his throat. "I don't think whoever is on the other side of that door agrees with you."

"Who could it be? It's Christmas morning, for heaven's sake. Mom has the code—"

"9653," he murmurs.

I jerk up and glare at him.

Ruben glances down at the space I used to occupy then rubs his jaw and smiles. "You still use that?" He laughs. "I guess I can come over whenever I like."

"How did you know that?"

"Come on, Cadence. Everyone knew you were obsessed with *Twilight* in high school. I just didn't know you still were."

"I'm not. It's just a habit now, and one I'm going to change. It's already brought way too much trouble into my life." But with Axley snoring softly, the statement doesn't ring true.

The knocking continues and Ruben shakes his head. "Well, it isn't anyone who went to high school with you, or they would know to punch in W-O-L-F."

I groan. My obsession with Jacob was borderline pathetic, but he and Bella just made so much more sense. Who wants a moody vampire when you can have a good-hearted wolf? But Ruben Palmer is one thousand percent Edward. He's rich, popular, and pretty much the whole world is in love with him.. All he's missing is color-changing eyes and some bloodlust. "I have no idea who it is, but you'd better hide." I point to my bedroom door.

"Hide?"

"Do you want the whole world to know you spent the night here?"

"I doubt the whole world is behind that door, and frankly—" His head drops down to the arm of the couch. "I'm too tired to care."

"Your girlfriend might care."

His head lifts up at that. "Daphne doesn't—"

I wave his excuses away. I'm really not prepared to hear him talk about Daphne three seconds after extracting myself from his arms. I bend over and carefully lift Axley from his chest. Axley stretches, but doesn't wake. I practically kick Ruben's legs off the couch and shove him toward my room with my hip. He shakes his head as if he's disappointed in me, but finally stumbles toward the door. I follow behind him with Axley in my arms. My legs ache from being scrunched up all night. Based on Ruben's small, unsteady steps, he must be feeling even worse. He stops when we reach my room, and I walk around him to open the door with my free hand. His hair needs a comb, his sweater isn't laying right, and his jaw has grown the length of stubble that a woman wants to catch under her fingernails. But the worst thing about Ruben is his eyes. They're blurry, hazed, and filled with a devil-may-care gleam, like nothing in the world could disturb him.

He shakes his rumpled head, which does nothing to clear that look from his eyes, and puts his arms out. "Do you want me to take Axley?"

"No, I'll keep him. Just get in there and stay quiet." I shut my bedroom door in his face, then turn and prop Axley closer to my chest.

What if it's Moira? It can't be, right? She would have just let herself in. Still, my feet stop moving, no longer willing to take the last few steps. Lowering my head, I take in Axley's scent. It's different from when he first got here. His hair smells like apricots and cream, because every time I go to the store I forget to buy baby shampoo. I hold completely still and get the slightest scent of coconut from the fancy face lotion I bought while I was in Vietnam.

If Moira is off the show and behind that door, will she take him away? When would I see him again? Axley smells like me now. I should have some visitation rights for that, at least.

I shake my head and force my feet to move forward. Axley is Moira's child. Moira's. I have absolutely no right to him, nor does a child really fit into my life right now. I've already lost my job once because of him.

I've also gotten my job back because of him, but still...

I take a deep breath, and right after three sharp knocks that jostle Axley awake, I open the door.

It isn't Moira.

"Ben?"

Ben's eyes flick to mine briefly, then slide down to Axley. His thick gray eyebrows raise, his mouth opens, but no words come out.

How am I going to explain Axley to Ben? He isn't just Ruben's grandfather, he's practically a grandfather to me. Of all the people I don't want to lie to, he's probably at the top of the list.

"Cadence." Ben's voice is soft, and a little wistful. "Welcome back to Rosco. I should have come to see you earlier."

I resist the urge to look at the clock on my microwave. Perhaps he could have come earlier in the week, but any earlier in the day and it still would have been dark outside. "I should have come to see you as well. Won't you come in?"

I open the door wide and Ben crosses the threshold, but doesn't go any farther. He clears his throat and shakes his head slowly. "First things first, I suppose. Merry Christmas, Cadence."

"Merry Christmas to you as well." I've only been awake for a few minutes, but I'm pretty certain no other Christmas will ever top this one in strangeness—first my waking up in Ruben's arms, then his grandfather standing here while Ruben hides in my bedroom.

Ben takes two steps toward my living room and then turns back around. He obviously wants to say something, but doesn't. Is this about my Laos project? Could he be here to tell me they finally see its merits and they're greenlighting it? After getting my job back, I'd finally got a few people to pay attention to it. Even though they acted as if they'd only vaguely heard of it before. It was nice to be back at corporate where I could look people in the eyes and tell them my ideas instead of trusting them to read my emails.

"Would you like something to eat?" I ask feebly.

Ben waves his hand to the side. "No, thank you. You know I see you as family, right?"

I nod. "I think of you the same way."

His lips press together, but he doesn't seem angry, just... disappointed? Maybe hurt, even. "Then why have you been keeping your baby a secret?"

"I haven't been..." I stop, because I guess I have been keeping Axley a secret, but not on purpose. Ben's eyes are focused like lasers on Axley, currently sitting on my hip. How did he even find out? "Ruben told you?"

"No," Ben's voice hardens. "Ruben did *not* tell me. I tried calling him this morning and he didn't answer."

Axley makes a small noise in his throat that can only be

described as a gurgle. He must be getting hungry. I need to make him a bottle, but I can't exactly turn away Ruben's grandfather and the founder of Palmer Hotels one minute after he arrived. "Would you like to sit down? I need to make Axley breakfast."

"Axley." Ben sighs the name as if it were the most beautiful thing he's ever heard.

The world shifts at his approval. Something must be very wrong.

I haven't seen Ben since I arrived in Rosco, but Ruben would have told me if he was starting to have memory or comprehension problems. He's in his seventies, but he's always been healthy, and in better shape than most men in their fifties.

I motion for Ben to sit on the sofa. Wrapping paper still litters the floor, and both my mug and Ruben's are sitting on the coffee table. Maybe he'll think those were Axley's and mine? Or that I'm a complete slob? As long as he doesn't deduce that his grandson is sitting in my bedroom with only a hollow door between us, he can think what he wants.

Ben doesn't seem to notice the state of my living room as he sits down, his eyes never leaving Axley. "Can I hold him for you while you make his breakfast? Please?"

My fingers itch to text Ruben and ask if Ben is okay. But sometime during the night, my phone died and...oh crap. Ruben's phone is sitting on the coffee table. It's slim and sleek with no case. Seriously, how rich do you have to be to have no case on your phone? Today I'm counting it as luck. An uncovered phone could belong to anyone.

I bring Axley over and set him beside Ben on the couch. The kitchen looks into the living room. With Ben sitting down, I'll be able to see the two of them. Ben immediately lifts Axley from under his shoulders and stands him up on the cushion. "Let me get a look at you," he says, and I take the opportunity to quickly slip Ruben's phone behind my back and edge into the kitchen. "He doesn't look much like you."

"No," I call over my shoulder, even though I'm a bit miffed at his comment. Sure, Axley and I share no DNA, but I think his ears look a bit like mine. "I think he takes after his father."

Ben's face splits into a large grin. "He does, doesn't he?"

Seriously, what is wrong? If I could just sneak into my bedroom, I could ask Ruben, but I'm not quite ready to leave Ben alone with Axley without knowing his condition. Instead, I plug in my phone. Mom will know if Ben has gone downhill health wise in the last few years. I can text her.

I turn on the sink and wait for the water to get warm enough for me to mix Axley's formula. Ben is making cooing sounds at Axley like he's a newborn. Axley is blinking up at Ben as if transfixed, and Ben's eyes are shining, the smile on his face one of pure enjoyment.

Sheesh. Ruben should probably get to work making great-grandbabies. Ben looks like he's in heaven. I can't remember the last time I've seen him so happy.

I'm filling the bottle when my phone comes to life. It immediately pings once. Then twice, and then several more times. How many people are wishing me a Merry Christmas?

I pick up my phone. The first text is from Emily. Man, I miss her. Why did she have to move?

> You and Ruben??? What have you been up to while out of the country??? Text me. NOW.

What the heck? I click on the next message. This one is from an old high school friend who only had my number because I helped her plan our five-year class reunion.

> Congratulations! I knew there was something between the two of you at the reunion. It was so obvious, the way Ruben kept looking at you.

The next one is from Rebecca and my heart sinks. Whatever has gotten into everyone is affecting my coworkers as well.

> Congratulations! I didn't even know you and
> Ruben were dating. And your baby is adorable!
> I hope the three of you have a very Merry
> Christmas!

Our baby? Like, Axley? My heart pounds as I scan message after message on my phone. I don't bother opening any more until I see my mom's message.

> You'd better look at People's website and then
> let me know what to tell everyone who keeps
> messaging me. Also, we need to get you some
> curtains.

I set Axley's bottle on the counter and navigate to *People*. My phone flashes and I curse under my breath. I'm there. Not just me, but me and Ruben *and* Axley, asleep on the couch. My head is resting on Ruben's chest like it knows what it's doing and Axley is snuggled up between us like he belongs there. Ruben's right arm is draped over my bare shoulder and his left is encircling both me and Axley, keeping both of us from rolling off the couch.

We are the picture of domestic bliss. Beneath us is a title in red letters.

Ruben Palmer's Secret Family, Unwrapped on Christmas!

I grab the counter for support and quickly scan the article, as well as a few others. My name is never mentioned, and it's easy to see from the conjecture of multiple "sources" that nobody actually knows anything. Conjecture has us hiding out in Rosco, since Ruben rarely has media following him here. Others claim that I've been extorting him for money. They could have taken one look at the small apartment and lack of window coverings and known that wasn't happening. Basically the article's only substance is the picture. Nothing else is concrete. I loosen my grip on the counter. Ruben is a playboy with a different woman at least every year. This might just blow over?

Maybe?

Ruben will definitely have some explaining to do with Daphne, but I can help him. It isn't like she'll be intimidated by me in my 15-year-old sweatshirt. Everything about Ben's strange behavior snaps into place. He isn't becoming senile—he thinks Ruben and I have been hiding a grandson from him.

Why in heaven's name would we do that?

My bedroom door cracks open and Ruben's eyes scans the scene. When he catches sight of Ben, he throws open the door. "Grandpa, I thought I heard you. What are you doing here?"

Ben stiffens, and all the joy that has been practically rolling off of him melts away. Why in the world did Ruben leave my room? It's the last thing we need.

"Ruben." Ben's voice is hard. "This is where you've been all morning? I should have known."

"How could you have known?" Ruben hasn't picked up on Ben's tone. He jaunts over to the couch, ruffles Axley's dark hair, and then sits next to Ben. "Merry Christmas."

"Merry Christmas?" Ben pulls Axley closer to him. "I suppose it is a Merry Christmas, but I might have missed out on it if it were up to you."

Ruben rubs a hand down his face like he's trying to keep up. "I'm sorry, did I miss something?"

"Are you deliberately trying to hurt me? You know how much I've always loved Cadence. Why would you keep this from me?"

Ruben slides away from Ben and looks him up and down. "Keep what from you? Of course I know you love Cadence, but don't read anything into me being here. I accidentally fell asleep on the couch. Nothing happened. Don't get your hopes up."

"Don't get my hopes up?" Ben looks down at Axley and back at Ruben.

Ruben has zero clue what he has just walked into. I try to

wave at him, but his eyes are trained on Ben. I've never seen Ben so livid, and I get the feeling Ruben hasn't either.

Ben stands up with Axley still in his arms. "If you think I won't get my hopes up, you're wrong, young man. I have no idea why you and Cadence have chosen to keep Axley a secret from me, but it stops now. I'll have him in my life whether you like it or not. All your philandering has to stop. It's high time you settled down."

Philandering? I press my lips together to stop a laugh. It is a pretty good description of Ruben's dating life, even if it's a word that hasn't been used in the past fifty years. Ruben stands, both hands on his hips. He looks as if he's about to lash out at Ben, and Ben looks like he'll welcome it. I won't have it. Not on Christmas.

"Ben," I say. "I think there's been a misunderstanding. Let me explain."

Ben's face softens as he turns to me. "No, Cadence, you don't need to explain anything. I've been telling Ruben for years he needs to settle down, and he has always known how much I hoped he'd settle down with you." Ben's voice catches and my eyes flash to Ruben, but he's focused on the floor, his jaw set. "I don't know why he's asked you to hide your relationship from me, but that's something I will take up with him at home. Thank you for letting me see Axley." His smile drops and he turns to Ruben. "Ruben, I expect to see you within the hour."

Ben walks into the kitchen and kisses Axley on the top of his head before handing him to me. "Merry Christmas, Cadence." He places a soft kiss on my forehead. It's the closest thing to a kiss from my Dad I've had in fifteen years, full of pride and familial devotion. A lump forms in my throat. "You have given me the best gift imaginable."

I take Axley but don't move. Ruben is stuck in place as well, glancing between Ben, Axley, and me.

Ben lets himself out without any of us saying a word.

"So…" I have no idea what to say. "Time to stop your philandering, eh?"

My sad attempt at a joke doesn't even register on Ruben's face. He shakes his head. "What was that all about? Does my grandfather often visit you?"

"Um, no. Today was a special occasion."

"Christmas?"

"No. At least, not just Christmas." I pull his phone from my back pocket. "You might want to look at your messages. Or any internet site or social media app."

He takes his phone and swipes it open. His eyebrow's raise, and I assume he's shocked at the number of notifications on his phone. But before he has a chance to click anything, his phone rings.

He curses under his breath, but answers it.

"Hey, Andrew, Merry Christmas." Ruben's voice sounds anything but merry. It sounds exhausted. How much sleep was he actually able to get on that sad excuse for a couch? I can't understand the words coming out of the phone, but I can hear the tone. Someone is either very upset or very excited.

Ruben rubs his forehead. "I don't even know what you're talking about. Has the whole world gone crazy?"

I open the *People* article and put my phone in front of Ruben's face. His eyes fly to my uncovered window and back to the couch before meeting mine. "I'll call you back," he says, ignoring the frantic voice on the other end of the line, and ends the call. He takes my phone from my hand and his shoulders drop. "Oh, Cadence, I'm so sorry." His eyes close tight. "I really didn't mean to get you mixed up in anything. Are you going to be okay?"

"Me?" I ask. He should be worried about Ben and Daphne, and whatever troubles this is going to cause the company. "I'm going to be fine."

"But they got Axley too."

At that I curse, because the last thing Moira and Axley need is for the whole world to know about the two of them. "Well, that is unfortunate, but there isn't really anything to be done about it now. I'm more worried about Ben."

I can see the wheels turning in his head as he looks from me to Axley, then back to the door where Ben just left. He curses again. "So Grandpa thinks…" He runs a hand through his rumpled hair but doesn't seem to be able to finish the sentence.

"He thinks Axley is yours." All of Ruben's nervous motions stop. "He said he looks like you."

Ruben swallows and closes his eyes, as if in pain. "I have to tell him."

"Good luck with that. He seems to like the idea."

"If you only knew." He grimaces. "Grandpa has been trying to set me up with you since the fourth grade. This is going to break his heart."

I have no response. When our families have gathered together, there were always a few gentle prods from both sides, but Ruben never took them seriously and neither did I. The last thing any teenager wants is to go out with someone their family wants them to date. "How can they print that picture? We're in the privacy of my home. Can we make them retract it?"

"Retracting won't change the fact that the world has seen this photo. And we were visible from the street. Legally, that's all the cameraman needs to explain there wasn't an expectation of privacy. Sorry, I should have thought of that. I'm not used to anyone taking pictures of me in Rosco." Ruben grabs his shoes and dashes to the door. "I have to go." He pauses before opening it and turns to look at me. "What a start to Christmas, eh? I get to obliterate my grandpa's favorite Christmas present ever." He drops his shoes, takes a few steps back toward me, and takes Axley's hand. "I'd be proud if you were mine, buddy. But I can't let my grandpa think something that isn't true. I hope you have a very merry Christmas."

He looks at me and, for a moment, seems as if he's about to lean down and kiss me on the forehead like Ben did. Like we're an old married couple and this is our routine before he's off to work.

"Merry Christmas, Ruben." I lean forward and give him a hug, because a hug makes sense between us, and married couple kisses absolutely do not. "Let me know if you need any help talking to Ben."

Ruben nods and leans forward, his face serious. "If he gets too upset, I'll just tell him Axley *is* mine, then force you to make an honest man out of me."

A strange sensation leaps in my chest, but I tap it down. Yesterday I thought maybe I could hang out with "just Ruben," but this morning made it very clear that "just Ruben" doesn't exist. The man in front of me is, and always will be, Ruben Palmer, heir presumptive to the Palmer Hotel empire. "Ha ha. I'm pretty sure Daphne would love that."

"I'm not that worried about Daphne at the moment. In fact, she might be the one who sent the paparazzi."

"What?"

He shakes his head. "I don't know who else could have done it. I was supposed to be in New York last night."

"With Daphne?" I don't like the way her name feels in my mouth.

"Yes. There was a party we were going to attend, and, well…" He runs his hands through his hair. "I told her I couldn't make it. And I haven't really made it to any of our dates the past two weeks."

"Why would that make her send people here to take pictures?"

He turns and starts to slip his shoes on. "She joked that I've been absent because of a woman." Then he shakes his head. "But it was a joke. I'm sure of it. Or at least I was yesterday."

A snort escapes my lips. "Well, don't worry too much about it. Nothing about this—" I flick my hand down, gesturing at my bedraggled look— "is going to worry Daphne VanPelt. The rest of the world is going to feel the same. I'm sure this will blow over nice and quick."

Ruben freezes in the middle of putting on his second shoe, then with a shake of his head, he slips it on. He opens my door and turns to me. My stupid sweatshirt has fallen off my shoulder again, and he steps toward me to pull it up. The feel of his fingertips along my shoulder and collarbone make me think wild things. Things like, maybe becoming the mother of Ruben's children isn't the craziest idea Ben has ever had.

I lift my chin and give myself a mental shake. Standing this close to Ruben would make any woman think that. It's just his stupid animal magnetism. Why did I ever question it?

Ruben's hand stays on my shoulder but I choose to ignore it. He probably doesn't even realize he's doing it. "Cadence, I only got a glimpse of that photo, but it's the sweetest picture anyone has taken of me since our sophomore history class. The world is going to go nuts over it—worse than the skins game pictures, for sure. If you think anyone's girlfriend could look at her man in a picture like that and not go berserk," he shrugs, "you are the one being preposterous."

My body reacts like it's a Christmas tree and someone just flipped on the lights. Ruben, you wretch. You can't do this to me. I channel all my energy into appearing bright and happy and unaffected by the fact that he has said the sweetest and most painful thing I've ever heard. "You really think so?" I make a face that probably looks like I walked in on one of Axley's more epic messes. Only this time, I'm the one causing all the problems. "Are you and Daphne going to be okay?"

"Daphne and I are fine. Don't worry, please. We aren't serious, at all." He grits his teeth together. "I'm going to need you to trust me on this one until I have time to talk to her and my lawyer. But believe me when I say she'll be just fine, as long as I don't have her arrested for sending the paparazzi. But I am worried about my grandpa." His hand on my shoulder squeezes. "And I'm worried about you."

"Me?"

"I hate that I've dragged you into this messy life of mine. But I'll fix it. I promise."

Messy life? Ruben's life is supposed to be perfect. "I'll be fine."

"Just promise me you won't run off to Vietnam again." Ruben's face is serious, but he's joking, right? I never ran off to Vietnam. He was the one who forced me to go. Almost twice. I furrow my brow and open my mouth to question his choice of words, but he puts his other hand on my other shoulder and bends down slightly so we're at eye level. The intensity of his dark eyes strikes differently than they did last night. Last night they were soft and almost fanciful. This morning they are hard and pragmatic. The magic of Christmas Eve didn't carry over to Christmas—not once the world saw me with Ruben. Those hard eyes narrow in concentration. "I can fix this, I promise. I don't want us to stop talking again. I've missed you too, and last night was…" He pauses like he's trying to find the right word. "Nice."

Nice.

I mean, it *was* nice, but is that such a hard word to come up with?

He drops his hands off my shoulders and strides out the door, shutting it behind him.

All the Christmas decorations in the world couldn't make my apartment feel full now that he's gone. I glance at the couch and our mugs. How did this all happen? What, exactly, was in that tea?

I glance out the window to make sure no one is out there taking pictures, but it looks like even the paparazzi want to spend Christmas morning with their families. As soon as the stores open after the holidays, I'm buying blinds.

Not that Ruben will be sleeping on my couch or even spending time here again. He may have promised to still talk to me, but I'm pretty sure having our faces plastered all over the internet is the end of our budding adult friendship. He said his relationship with Daphne isn't serious, but I've seen their pictures on the internet, and they are glued together..

And those pictures of the two of them kissing and snuggling together at nightclubs don't bother me because of Daphne. They bother me because of the little truth that's been banging around in the back of my head ever since Ruben first came to my apartment. People in Ruben's world touch, kiss, and have paternity problems all the time. It doesn't mean anything to them.

I, on the other hand, thought lacing our arms together on Axley's stroller might have had astronomical significance.

I saw the look in his eyes as he left. He'll do anything to get this story buried. Which means we're done. Just like when I left three years ago, he's going to cut me out and go on with his life like I was never in it.

Because I never really have been. Not in any way that mattered.

CHAPTER
THIRTEEN

alf an hour later, Mom rushes into my apartment. I'm wearing the Christmas pajamas I'd meant to change into last night. Axley has a matching pair and when Mom walks in, I hand one to her too.

"What's this?" she asks.

"I got us matching pajamas." Mom smiles. We haven't had matching Christmas pajamas since I was a kid and Dad was still alive. I chalk this up to one more magical thing about having Axley here. "I know we need to talk, but Axley and I have been waiting until you got here to dig into his stocking."

Mom tips her head to one side and nods, taking the pajamas and heading to the bathroom to change. When she comes out we're all wearing red thermals with llamas in Christmas hats all over them.

"You look fantastic," I say.

"We all do," Mom says with a smile. "Thank you."

We help Axley get everything out of his stocking. Once he's happily munching on his Christmas-tree-shaped yogurt melts, mom turns to me. "Tell me what's going on with you and Ruben. How did he end up on your couch?"

"He came over to give Axley a present, and we fell asleep

watching TV." It sounds so innocent when I say it that way. "When we woke up, the world had gone crazy." Merry Christmas, Ruben. I got you a public scandal.

Mom shakes her head. "That's all? You could have told me that the moment I set foot in the door. I'm sure it will all blow over. Ben has whole teams that work on stuff like this. Besides, it's Christmas. Maybe no one will see the article. Who spends time on their phones and computers on Christmas?"

I sigh. "Literally everyone, Mom. There's no point in getting an amazing Christmas present or overdecorating your tree if you can't post it on social media. And it isn't just one article. That picture is everywhere."

Mom sighs in return. "Well, at the very least we need to get away from our phones. I'm leaving mine in the kitchen. There's nothing to be done about it now. And it's not like this is Ruben's first scandal." She brushes her hands together like that's the end of it.

Mom is right about needing to admit this is out of our hands and enjoy Axley's first Christmas, but I know this scandal is going to be a big headache for Ruben. He's never been one to cheat. His splits have always been amicable, and he waits just long enough to start dating the next woman so that, although seen as a womanizer, he's one that people don't actually get mad at. It's more like they're all secretly hoping he'll keep making the rounds until he ends up with them. This photo is going to change all of that.

Mom grabs Axley and ruffles his hair. "Should we see what presents Santa brought you?"

The subject is closed. Mom never even asked if I'm dating Ruben, or if I'm thinking about it. Well, why would she? The two of us make no sense. Still, she could have been a little curious about the situation. She's my mom. She's allowed to be delusional about my romantic prospects.

I rub my forehead like I can rewire some of the crazy thoughts of the past week. It's time for a little Christmas magic.

I'd gotten a sneak peek of the adorableness of Axley opening presents, and Mom is going to love it.

By Axley's second gift he's figured out the whole wrapping paper system like a pro. Mom and I both snap way too many pictures of him. Then Mom opens her gift from Ruben—the tiny, professionally wrapped one. Her eyes go wide as she lifts the dainty gold chain from the box. A single charm dangles from the end. It's an apple. It's perfect.

She opens my presents next—a few hand-tailored shirts and dresses—and seems almost as happy with them as she was with her apple necklace. Almost.

I finish opening my presents next. A lot of them are things to make my life easier with Axley. The biggest is a cuddle sleeper designed to give Axley his own space in my bed. I never told Mom my anxiety about buying a crib, but she must have felt it.

When we're done, I pull out some fruit and cheese while Mom rests on the couch. I've avoided looking at the sofa as much as possible, which is tough in an apartment as small as mine. Axley is playing with the cars Ruben brought him while Mom keeps tugging at the apple charm around her neck. The man apparently knows how to give a gift. Maybe that's why none of his girlfriends talk badly about him after they break up. It would taint the memory of the man who gave them their favorite dictionaries.

I snort at the thought of Daphne VanPelt looking happy at receiving a dictionary from him. He probably sends her super impersonal gifts, like diamonds every other Friday.

Sucks to be her.

My phone vibrates on the counter next to me. It's the gift-giver himself.

"Hello?" I answer.

"Merry Christmas." His voice is low and sensual—his cologne commercial voice. Why is he using his cologne commercial voice on me? Can't he be normal? My brain can't handle it. I don't live in his world of harmless flirtations. Mom looks up at me and I cover the receiver and whisper his name to her. Then I sneak into my bedroom like I'm in high school, hiding away when a boy calls.

Daphne has nothing on me in the sophistication department.

I close the door and fall onto my bed. All I need is braces and a high ponytail and I'd be the poster child for teen romance. "I'm pretty sure you already wished me a Merry Christmas this morning," I say in what I would like to think would be *my* cologne commercial voice. He doesn't respond—doesn't even make a sound. Ugh. Why can't *I* be more normal? I switch to a professional tone. "How's Ben? Did he take the news alright?" I don't dare ask about Daphne.

"Grandpa is…" He lets out a small puff of air. "Well, he would like you and Axley to come over for Christmas dinner. Your mom too."

"Why?"

"Your family is like family to ours. We had your mom over for dinner plenty of times while you were in Vietnam."

"On holidays?"

"Sure." I can almost hear his shrug. Liar.

"Which holidays?"

"I'm 95% sure she came over for Groundhog's Day last year."

"Are you being serious?"

"No. I mean, maybe she did. The point is, it isn't weird for the three of you to come over today. And Grandpa may need to hear a few things from your own mouth."

I don't like the sound of that. "What do you mean?"

"I guess someone sent him an anonymous note this morning saying they had proof that I was the father. All they want is a hundred thousand dollars to hand it over to him. Obviously that's a scam, and I told him as much. But it doesn't help that he thinks Axley looks like me."

No one could have proof that Ruben is the father. That note has to be a scam. The only person who even thinks that is…crap.

Maybe this is all my fault after all, and not just because I haven't invested in blinds. "Have you talked to Daphne?"

"Andrew has. They're working some things out."

"Who is Andrew, again?"

"My publicist. You know him. He was two years older than us in high school."

Andrew Lincoln. I vaguely remember him. "Did she admit to sending the photographer?"

"No, and I'm inclined to believe her."

I sigh. "I think I know who took the picture and sent the note."

There's a creak on the other line. Is Ruben in his bed too? It sounds like he just sat up. "Who?"

"Christian."

"Why would Christian Rasmussen think I'm the father of your baby?" There is no trace of cologne in his voice now.

Ugh. Could this conversation be more embarrassing? "He jumped to his own conclusions after reading your email over my shoulder."

"And you let him think..." Ruben trails off. "I mean, not that I wouldn't want . . ."

"I was upset with him and didn't take time to explain. I'm sorry. I should have. I will."

"The damage is done now. I hope he got a pretty penny for that picture, because it's costing him his job. I'll take care of him. You don't need to speak to or see him again unless you want to."

"Oh, but you do? This is my fault, Ruben. If I had just told him..."

"Being in the media is kind of my thing. It isn't yours."

"Yeah, well, you're not the one with a baby."

"Tell that to my grandpa. He thinks..."

His pause lasts long enough that I have to prod him. "What does he think?"

"Well, he thinks that perhaps I'm trying to keep the two of you all to myself. Something about how I have to share everything else with the world, so he can understand why I would hide you from the media. But he's pretty upset at the thought that I kept you from him and my parents."

I laugh.

"It isn't funny." His voice is hard.

"It's a little bit funny."

"I'm glad you think so. Why don't you come over for dinner, then? You're sure to have a good chuckle."

"But what if someone sees me going there? Do you *want* the world to get more documentation about your ladylove and secret child?"

He sighs. "That depends."

"Depends on what?"

"Which of my secret families are you talking about? You and Axley? Sure. It will deflect from my real secret family that I keep hidden in Australia."

I smile. This is territory I'm comfortable with. Joking. "Why would you keep your secret family in Australia? Flights there are horrific."

"Ah, but the time difference is so convenient. Next year I can spend Christmas day there, hop on a horrific flight, and still make it in time for Christmas dinner in Rosco."

"Sounds like you've thought through everything."

"I'm nothing if not meticulous. Now, will you come for dinner? It would really help my Australian family."

"Fine."

"Fine," he says back, and I hang up the phone before I can change my mind.

I open the door and tell Mom, "It looks like we're having Christmas dinner with the Palmers."

CHAPTER
FOURTEEN

Ben has always loved me. He got me my first internship when I was in high school, wrote an amazing reference letter when I applied to college, and made sure I was snatched up by Palmer Hotels the minute I graduated. I'm used to the glimmer that lights his eyes when he sees me, but the way he keeps glancing across the dinner table at me, Axley, and Ruben is next level. He could light fireworks with the sparks coming from his eyes.

Ruben wasn't lying when he said Ben hadn't believed him.

Even Mom is starting to look at us questioningly, and she *knows* Axley isn't my child, let alone Ruben's.

Ruben's parents are here for Christmas, and I can't remember the last time I saw them. They spent a lot of Ruben's high school years in Colorado on a small cherry orchard. Ben chose to sell his apple orchard to my grandparents, but Ruben's parents went back to their farming roots. Funny how things like that happen. The last thing I wanted to do was grow apples, and the last thing Ben's parents wanted to do was operate a hotel chain. I never heard why Ruben stayed in Rosco with Ben when they left, even though I'd always been curious.

Ruben's mom and dad haven't said much. They're probably

waiting for conclusive evidence before they show excitement or disappointment. I don't think any of them would be as suspicious if it weren't for the fact that Axley's coloring really does look more like Ruben's than mine. Curse Moira and her amazingly dark hair.

The only other person at the table besides my family and the Palmers is Andrew. He'd been one of Ruben's best friends during our sophomore year, but I hadn't seen him since he graduated. Doesn't he have a family of his own he should be spending Christmas with? Did I ruin another person's Christmas by allowing Christian to think Ruben was Axley's dad?

We make it to dessert—a chocolate custard that looks divine but will totally ruin Axley's best shirt—before Ben brings up the elephant in the room. "I suppose you know that Ruben told us Axley isn't his."

"Yes. And it's true." I take a bite of custard, hoping it signals the end of the conversation.

But Ben isn't deterred. "Then why have you been hiding him?"

"I haven't been hiding him."

Ben raises an eyebrow and turns to Mom. "Ruth, did you know about Axley when he was born?"

I put a hand on Mom's arm. She *hates* lying, she's terrible at it, and she didn't find out about Axley until after Moira took off on that plane. "Mom found out about Axley almost as soon as I did." Mom's shoulders relax.

Ben sets down his spoon. "Then why didn't you tell us about him? If Ruben had a child—and I'm not convinced he doesn't—you know I would be showing everyone his picture. You didn't even mention Axley."

Mom straightened. "It's not like we see each other every day, Ben."

If Ben heard what Mom said, he didn't show it. "And just look at his coloring. His hair is exactly the color of Ruben's, and mine, for that matter."

"Your hair is gray," Mom answers as if that proves anything. She's floundering, and I'm tired of everyone saying Axley doesn't look like me. He's as much mine as anyone else's in this room. I make his bottle every morning and sleep next to him every night.

"He has my ears," I say with determination, lifting my chin. "His ears look exactly like mine."

Mom blinks and turns to Axley. His hair is floppy, so half of his ear is covered. She pulls up the dark locks, looks under them, and looks at me. I tuck my light brown hair behind my ear and jut it out for everyone to see.

Mom smiles. "They do look a bit like yours, don't they?"

They really do. We both have a perfect curve at the top of our ears, no bumps or points or anything, and they poke out from the head just the right amount.

Mom is shaking her head like she can't believe it, but then stops and her smile disappears. "Oh, this is ridiculous," Mom mutters under her breath to me. "We just need to tell them."

I shake my head and motion to Andrew. Andrew would jump at any chance to clear Ruben's name. If we told them the truth, Moira would be kicked off her show, for sure.

My phone buzzes for what seems like the thousandth time today. I've mostly ignored it, but I hate the direction this conversation is going, so I pull it out. I don't recognize the number.

> I'm calling you right now. Please answer. I won't have much time to talk. —Darling.

What the heck? Did someone leak my number? Who ends a text with the word darling? Shouldn't that be at the beginning? Assuming someone would call me darling at all. Putting it at the end makes it look like a signature.

Darling.

The word jolts a memory inside me. *Wendy Moira Angela Darling.* It's Moira. Garff called her darling all the time. Mom and I did too sometimes. Who would have thought we'd need our silly Peter Pan references someday so she could text me about her secret baby on Christmas?

My phone buzzes again, and this time it's her number calling. "I'm sorry, I have to take this."

Mom raises her eyebrows and I mouth "Moira" to her. Her eyes widen and she pushes me out of the chair.

Every eye is on me as I walk out of the room.

Just before I escape the dining room, Mom clears her throat. "See, I told you Ruben isn't the father. He's calling now."

I spin around. Why would she say that? I told Ruben that Axley's father was dead. My eyes meet his and I panic. "No, it isn't, Mom."

Both Andrew's and Ben's eyes grow sharp.

"Who's on the phone, then?" Andrew asks.

Mom laughs and it's the falsest thing I've ever heard. "Well, not his father, exactly. Someone like a father."

Oh. My. Gosh. Did Mom just decide to classify Moira as someone like a father to Axley?"

"What do you mean?" Ruben asks, but I can't answer. Moira is hissing on the other end of the phone like she's trapped in a prison camp and trying to break out.

Sounds like a dream compared to my reality right now.

I hold the phone close with both hands, covering it so I can whisper. "What is going on? Are you coming home?"

"No. That's not why I'm calling. I saw the news about you and Ruben."

Moira is calling for the first time since she dropped Axley off and *this* is what she wants to talk about? I want to scream. "There is nothing going on between me and Ruben Palmer." It isn't a scream, but I said it louder than I should have, and I can tell at least a few people at the table heard. I walk completely out of the dining room.

Moira continues like she didn't hear me. "Everyone thinks

Axley is his son. That's great. That's all I wanted to say. It's the perfect cover."

"What do you mean, cover?" I ask, quietly this time. "I'm not going to make Ruben pretend to be Axley's father just so you can go on some dumb game show."

"It's a reality show and it isn't dumb. In fact, it's going really well. Better than I ever could have expected. Right away, the other ladies could tell I didn't have my life as put together, and they tormented me for a bit, but then Andre, well…he didn't like how they treated me and…I think I might win, Cadence. Andre is just so…so…" Her voice trails off and I can tell I'm losing her.

"Moira, Ruben doesn't want a son that isn't his. We're at his family's house now, trying to *convince* them that he isn't."

"Stop convincing them, then."

"Oh my gosh. It doesn't work that way. One DNA test will prove he isn't."

"You don't have the right to do a DNA test."

"Yeah, and how, exactly, am I going to explain that? And what will we tell them when you get back? 'Just kidding, we were lying the whole time. Not only is Axley *not* Ruben's child, but he isn't mine either.'"

Moira is silent.

"Moira?" She coughs. "Moira, you *will* be coming back. You have to."

"The Palmer family pretty much owes their success to your family. I'm sure they won't mind helping you out. Plus, Axley looked so happy in that photo. You know, we didn't even have a Christmas tree. You and Ruben can do so much better for him."

"There is no me and Ruben." I'm nearly shouting again, and I don't care. This is ridiculous. "They don't owe us anything. We bought their apple orchards two generations ago. What you're talking about is out of the question."

"I have to go."

"No. You can't go. Don't you want to talk to Axley? It's Christmas."

"No." Her voice cracks slightly on the word and it's the first time I think she might go through with her plan. "That will only make it harder. I'm not even supposed to have this phone. I snuck it from one of the field crew when I told him I found out my sister was dating Ruben Palmer. He totally let me use it after that. But Ruben might need to send him a signed picture. One of the muddy football ones—you know which ones I mean. After all this is over."

"No, wait—" But before I can say anything else there's a click and Moira is gone.

I stand there for a moment in a daze. Behind me, Mom is saying something about how the person on the phone really wanted to be in Axley's life but couldn't be right now but soon they would definitely want to be in Axley's life again, so...of course Ruben isn't the father.

Could this day get any worse? Christmas wasn't supposed to be like this. I want Christmas Eve back. Christmas Eve was lovely. I turn around and the first thing I see is Axley with custard all over his face and shirt, and I burst into tears.

Ruben is out of his seat before anyone else. His arms are around me instantly. "What happened?"

I glance up at his face, and I want to hide under the very expensive Turkish rug I'm standing on. Of course Moira would want him to take care of Axley. He looks like he could take on the world right now, and I'm half tempted to ask him to do it. I love Axley, but I'm not prepared to be a single mom forever.

Mom reaches me next. "What did *he* say?"

Moira is a *he* now. I get what she's saying but seriously, do we have to keep this up? Just for some stinking reality TV show?

Ruben's voice is soft. "Is he mad about the picture?"

I laugh. "No. Not mad at all."

Ruben's arms tense around me. "What do you mean?"

I wipe a tear that managed to escape my left eye and smile up at him. "*He . . .*" I make the same emphasis as Mom did as I glare at her. "Loved the picture. Is tickled pink about it." Mom grabs my phone as if there are answers in there. "He thinks Ruben should probably take care of me and Axley for the next three months *to life*."

Ruben stiffens, and I don't blame him. He glances at my phone. "Is he...in prison?"

Mom snorts and I shake my head because I'm pretty sure Moira is on some fancy beach ordering piña coladas and batting her eyes at some dude named Andre. "No, definitely not in prison."

Andrew clears his throat from the doorway to the dining room. "It isn't a bad idea." Everyone stares at Andrew, but no one says a word. The house is silent.

Ruben is the first to speak. "What isn't a bad idea?"

"I know most of you have been ignoring your phones today," Andrew says, "but a friend of Daphne's just put out a statement saying Ruben's relationship with Daphne has been fake. Her friend said she never understood why Daphne would agree to fake date anyone until she saw the photo of the three of you. Everyone is speculating that your past few relationships have just been a cover to protect your real family."

Ruben doesn't loosen his arms around me when he fires back, "What? Which friend?"

Andrew shrugs as if this mess is all in a day's work for him. "We can worry about that later. The thing is, the public loves it. They *want* this story to be true."

I wipe my face on Ruben's shirt and then turn to Andrew. "People want Ruben Palmer to be married to some nobody with a child?"

Andrew shakes his head. "Not a nobody." He pauses in a dramatic way only a salesman can. "His woman. His child."

"You cannot be serious," I say.

"But he is Ruben's child," Ben pipes up from the dining room.

"No, Grandpa, he's not." Ruben's chest rumbles while he talks. I don't think him holding me is helping Ben's grasp on

131

the situation. I straighten and Ruben lets his arms fall to his side.

Andrew paces. "That does complicate things."

"It complicates things?" I'm about to go ape wild all over this house. First Moira, and now Andrew, think Ruben should take responsibility for *Moira's* baby and I cannot deal with this anymore. "Ruben, how much do you trust Andrew?"

"Literally with my life."

I narrow my eyes at Andrew and he straightens. "Will you be able to keep whatever I tell you confidential?"

Andrew looks at Ruben. "I'm very proficient at keeping secrets."

I put a hand on one hip. "That isn't an answer."

"Yes, I will."

Okay. This ends now. I glance at Ben first, and then at the rock of a man beside me. "Ruben and I will not pretend Axley is our child. We can't. Axley isn't even *my* baby."

If I thought the silence was loud in the house before, now it's deafening. Ben shuffles forward after a moment and looks back at Axley, still happily making a mess of his custard in the antique high chair Ben either pulled out of storage or had delivered by helicopter on Christmas day. His gray eyebrows furrow and he shakes his head. "But…what about his ears?"

CHAPTER
FIFTEEN

After the briefest of meltdowns, considering the absolute insanity of our situation, Ben gets us all to sit back down at the table, where I finish explaining the whole story to everyone. Andrew, who has been taking notes, eyes me and Ruben. "I think the two of you need to talk. I'm ready to run with the story of your hidden family and fake relationships if you are. But I need your go-ahead."

I shake my head. "What do you mean, ready to run with the story? I just told you Axley isn't even mine."

Andrew nods. "But you also said Axley's mother wants this story to run."

Ruben has been mostly silent during my story. I'm not sure he's looked me in the eyes once since finding out I lied to him about Axley. But his eyes flash to mine now. "Andrew has an eye for this kind of thing. If he says this story will sell, it will sell."

I take a deep breath. "But why do we need a story? Won't this all go away once you get back together with Daphne, or find some other woman to date?"

Andrew taps his pen on his yellow legal pad. "Palmer Hotels relies on Ruben keeping up his popularity. You must realize that."

"But he doesn't have to always have a story, does he?"

"This story is already out. What I need to know is how we're going to spin it. Everyone loves the hidden family idea. If you're willing to participate and the boy's parents are willing, we can start now. We'll be careful not to outright say you *are* his hidden family. But we won't deny it either. People can make of it what they will. In the meantime, we'll get more photos of the two of you together and let social media do its work. If, for any reason, the truth comes out later on, down the road, we'll have deniability, since we never actually made a statement about it. No one is going to hate Ruben for treating someone else's child like his own. They won't hate you, either, for that matter."

Holy crap. Andrew wants to use the same deception technique I did. Maybe I should have been a publicist. But I didn't exactly love living my life that way, and I'm not about to sign up for more of it. "What if Daphne denies her friend's story?"

"She won't," Ruben answers.

I turn to him, but he's still looking down at his untouched custard. "How do you know she won't? Spurned women do all sorts of things."

Ruben eyes Ben, then says under his breath, "She won't deny her friend's story because there's nothing to deny. Can we talk privately? Now, perhaps?"

"Fine," I whisper back. "I'm not sure what you've been drinking, but her story is *not* true. You have not been hiding me and Axley for the past few years. I didn't even know about Axley until two weeks ago."

Ruben just smiles like I've said something perfectly normal to him, then asks everyone to excuse us.

I give Mom a look to make sure she'll watch Axley, but I needn't have bothered. I realized there wasn't a single person around that table who wouldn't protect him now. Even Andrew, who I can't imagine caring about anything other than getting his clients on the top trending charts, wouldn't let anything happen to Axley. He's his ticket to the front page.

Something inside me relaxes. Ruben and I aren't crazy enough to go through with Andrew's messed up plan, but I don't regret telling everyone what's been going on. Even if I hadn't been lying exactly, it's a relief to have a roomful of people who know the truth.

Ruben pulls my chair out like I'm the main character in a romantic comedy, and I get up and follow him. He opens the double doors to the den and motions for me to walk in first. Ben's house was always a favorite hang-out place for our friend group during high school. It's not modern or luxurious like the hotels he builds, but the rooms are large and welcoming, and there's room for a crowd.

The old sofas in the den have been replaced by one massive U-shaped sectional, and the carpet is new since I was here last, but most of the pictures are in the same place. A huge photograph of the lake dominates one wall, and the other holds a massive flat-screen TV.

Ruben motions for me to sit on one side of the sectional. I sink in and can't help but think this would have been a much better place to fall asleep with him last night.

I rub my head. Was that really only last night?

He takes a spot nearby, just far enough away that our legs don't touch. I run my hand along the cushions. "Next time we fall asleep on a couch together, let's make it this one. It's so much more comfortable than mine."

Ruben smiles, and for the first time in what feels like ages, he locks eyes with me. "I don't know if you've seen the pictures, but you looked quite comfortable."

I punch him softly in the arm and he pretends to be injured. I snort. "I didn't hurt you. You're such a faker."

"I am." Ruben rubs the spot on his arm, not like it's sore, but absentmindedly. "But I'm tired of it. I'm so sick of pretending. I want to be done with all of it."

"Oh, good. I don't want to pretend, either. Andrew's idea is bonkers."

Ruben stares forward. "That's not what I meant. And if you hate the idea, I really don't want you to do it. In fact, I'm not sure why we're even talking about this. I can find something else to keep the media talking. Maybe I can find a family of five somewhere who wants a fake father."

"I hear Australia is a good place to look."

I expect him to laugh, but instead he just nods and stands up, like our conversation is over. I pull him back down. "Somehow I don't think *that* would go over quite as well, now that you've already done it once." His hand goes back to rubbing his arm again. I barely touched him. I want to take his hand in mine to stop him, but I resist the urge. "Tell me what you mean."

He takes a deep breath. "I mean Daphne. And not just Daphne. Rachel, Acacia, Amira . . . all of them." He stops rubbing his arm and looks me in the eye. "The reason Daphne won't deny her friend's story is because it's true. We had a business arrangement, nothing more. And I gained over five hundred thousand followers because of it."

He doesn't talk about the followers like he's excited. He just looks tired, and I've never been more confused in my life. "Why would you date Daphne for followers?"

Ruben sighs and leans back into the sectional, stretching his legs onto the ottoman in front of us. "Do you remember what year my history picture went viral?"

"Of course. Sophomore year. You were basically a nobody, and then suddenly everyone was fainting over you. Even Ms. Webb, and she was like sixty-five."

"Do you remember anything else that happened that year?"

I shake my head. High school was pretty much a blur now, all melding into one big memory without solid moments, other than when Garff married mom and then divorced her. "I think our debate team made it to state that year."

Ruben chuckles softly. "I'm pretty sure you're right. That's not what I was thinking of, though. That was the year my parents moved to Colorado."

"It was?" I'd totally forgotten. Most of my memories of Ruben are from the time he lived here, in Ben's house. Our families have always been friends, but I don't remember hanging out at his parents' home. Only Ben's.

Ruben nods. "That year, a few news stories came out about my parents. Mom started feeling like she had to dress up every time she walked outside, and when she got tired of that stress, she stopped going outside much at all. Dad hated being known only for his last name. He just wanted to grow things. He never cared about the hotels. He wishes our family still had the orchard, and hates how many people are at the lake. He blames Grandpa for ruining one of the most beautiful places on earth."

Many of the locals felt the same way about Palmer Hotels. But Ruben's mom and dad did, too? "I didn't know."

Ruben shrugs like it's no big deal. "They're fine now. They love Colorado, and they've found a place that's almost as beautiful. But at the time, they were extremely unhappy with not just Grandpa, but with each other. Mom hated talking to reporters, but they were always calling. Dad just avoided phones and the public. And then my picture came out." He paused. "Do you know who took it?"

"It was going to be for the yearbook, wasn't it?"

"Yes. Andrew took it. He was on the yearbook committee that year. And as he was getting it ready to place it, all the girls kept asking to have a copy."

"Typical."

Ruben shook his head. "No. It wasn't typical. Do you even remember what I looked like before that photo? I'd only just gotten my height, but my weight hadn't caught up yet. I was scrawny and I'd only had my braces off for like three weeks."

"So it was the braces."

Ruben made a noise in his throat, which turned into a cough. "Yes, it was for sure the braces that gave me that smile. What else could it have been?" He shakes his head. "Anyway Andrew knew he had struck gold, because it wasn't a photo of just any dreamy-eyed 15-year-old, but a dreamy-eyed 15-year-old with the last name of Palmer. He talked to me about it, and the next time a reporter called, hoping to reach my parents, I asked them if they wanted a picture of me instead."

"Oh, Ruben." How have I never heard this story before?

"My parents stopped fighting. The hotels, which were doing well, but not at all like they are now, started booking up faster. Grandpa built two new hotels that year, and the income they started generating gave him enough money to send Mom and Dad a check that paid for a cherry orchard. Everything got better because of that one photo."

"And you didn't move to Colorado?"

"How could I? All of their media problems would have followed them if I had. But also, I didn't want to move. I love Rosco."

I swallow. That wasn't at all how I thought this story would end. "I didn't realize."

Ruben shrugged. "Most people don't. But if you graph the income and growth of Palmer Hotels, there's a huge jump that directly correlates to that one moment. And a few others as well."

"Skins football?" I ask innocently, like I've never typed it in a search bar.

"I think that series paid for the hotel in the Swiss Alps."

I'd been working in Vietnam then, but I still kept tabs on all of Palmer's new projects. I mentally pull out a calendar. He's right. Of course he's right. Holy crap. Could an amazing smile and perfect abs really do that? "So you really do have million-dollar abs."

"More like one hundred million, but yes." I suck in a breath. Is he serious? He isn't smiling. He's just sitting there calmly, as if earning a hundred million dollars from a few photos wasn't a big deal. "I'm not sure those pictures were worth it, though. Some of the things people have photoshopped out of them..." He shudders.

"But the hotel in the Alps is a masterpiece. You definitely helped out the family there." I smile at him. "And probably a few lonely housewives as well."

He glares at me, but one corner of his mouth turns up. "What about lonely development team members in Vietnam?"

I tip my head to one side and give him a face I hope is cute. "Oh, did you take off your shirt to help lonely employees in distant lands? How noble."

He raises his eyebrow. "Well, did it help?"

Did I look at those pictures from time to time? Sure. But like a scientist, not a voyeurist. It's an interesting thing to watch a man grow from an awkward teenager to a Greek god in front of a camera, and I can tell you one thing: Ruben Palmer's abs did not look like that in high school. "I was alone, and hardly knew anyone over there when those pictures came out. I might have looked at them. They reminded me of home."

"If I'd known you were that lonely, I could have sent you some pictures personally." He tips his head toward me with a wink. "You know, just to remind you of home."

There's a silent moment where I'm *not* imagining what type of shirtless photos Ruben might have sent me if this were a different world—a world where he had sent me any kind of correspondence at all. "Andrew would never allow pictures like that to float around without taking full advantage of them. I'd probably get sued for selling company secrets."

"Only if you sold them."

"You think I wouldn't, after you just told me how much they were worth?"

"They're worth that much to the company, but not to the owner of the picture. The whole company does better when my name is trending."

"Geez, Ruben. So all this time I thought you were making executive decisions, but really your job at Palmer hotels is just to smile at the camera and take off your shirt?"

He sticks his tongue out at me, and I'm suddenly regretful I hadn't allowed myself to be more childish with him. "I do make *some* decisions." He sighs. "But Grandpa trusts your assessment of locations more than mine. So, yes, being a hot topic item is an important job of mine. And I take it seriously. Seriously enough to only date women who can help build my fan base, and seriously enough to not get emotionally involved with any of them. That way, when we break it off, there's no damage to either of our reputations."

What can I say to that? I've been living a lie for two weeks and it has nearly killed me. Ruben has been doing it since high school. "I didn't know."

"You weren't supposed to." He rubs the back of his neck. "My family doesn't even know. They know I'm not super serious about the women I date, and they know I want the followers and notoriety that comes from dating them. But they think I like it, and I'd like to keep it that way." He looks at me. "But I made one really big mistake. I pulled you and Axley into this mess, and I'm not sure how to fix it."

Mess? This mess is Ruben's life. His perfect smile and perfect outings—all for show. But wait. "Are you telling me *none* of your relationships were real?"

"Andrew arranged all of them."

I sit up straighter and turn so I can see his face better. "What about Alyssa Fourtuna?"

His eyes widen and the corner of his mouth raises. "Okay, that was a little bit real." I grab a throw pillow and, well, throw it. It lands on his chest and he holds it tight. "What? Like you wouldn't date someone like her, if given the chance? She's…" Ruben's eyes glaze over slightly, and I really want to stick my tongue out, but apparently I'm still holding back. He has a point. The sample size of adults on the planet who would pass up the chance to put the moves on Alyssa would have a majority of coma patients in it. And a few of them would probably wake up for the opportunity. "Anyway," he shrugs, "it still didn't work out."

"Really?" I act surprised. "She didn't want to date someone who only wanted her for her body? Shocking."

Ruben sits up, his long legs sliding back up to a ninety-degree angle. His eyes catch mine. "Maybe *I* didn't want to date someone just for her body." I narrow my eyes at him because his answer still has to be sexist, right? I try to figure out how, but the low tone of his voice makes me feel like someone needs to put brighter light bulbs in this room. He tips his head to one side. "But you're right, too. It was mutual. And from then on, I just didn't bother to actually date the women I was linked to. They were all nice, but…"

I want him to finish that sentence so badly my teeth hurt. But what?

He leans toward me and I resist the urge to pull back. "I'm so sick of all the pretending." There are shadows under his eyes. He looks…vulnerable. He is a puppy every woman in the world would pick up and bring home to take care of. His voice is delicious and his face only a foot away from mine. "What I really want is something real."

Dang, he's good. I'm suddenly very much in the market for a puppy. There's no way all of those women who dated him didn't hope something more could come of it. "And you think because I live in your hometown, have a real job, and come with a baby, I'm more real."

"Hey." Ruben looks mortally wounded. "Creating and selling handbags is a real job."

"What about dancing on viral videos?"

"It's called choreography, and don't disparage it. Melinda worked hard on every single one of those."

"I have a hard time believing anyone is going to get excited about you dating me. I'm pretty basic, and I supposedly have a kid."

"Andrew has never been wrong about anything like this. If he thinks dating a mom is even more exciting than dating a supermodel, he's right. And like I said, I could do with a change."

"You want to trade in your baboon-butt hair scarf for a minivan?"

"My what?"

"Your baboon-butt hair scarf." I scoff like he's an idiot if he doesn't have one. "I hear they're all the rage."

He narrows his eyes at me. "No, they aren't. If they were, Andrew would have one for me. Besides, I don't need to trade in anything. The company has a van."

"I don't mean one of those fancy converted monster vans with tinted windows. I mean sliding doors and popcorn smashed between the seats."

"Do they sell them with popcorn already smashed between the seats?"

"If they're used, I don't think it's optional."

"So, if I buy a used minivan with child dirt, will you agree to date me?"

I laugh. "You mean fake date you?"

His answer takes a minute, and when it comes, it's a whisper. "Real…fake…whatever you want, Cadence. I'll do whatever you want."

And there it is. An invitation to uncharted territory. Ben wanted the two of us together like Mom wanted me to work for Palmers. But could we do it? For real? Was Ruben so tired of likes and followers that he was willing to *actually* date me? I want to ask him if we would be having this conversation if Andrew hadn't come up with the idea, or if Axley and I had been bad for his reputation.

What if the algorithms do change, and I become bad for him? He would have to move on, and I would have to let him. I'm not sure if I can do it. I open my mouth to say as much but he stops me by taking my hand.

"Before you answer, I want you to know that I have a pretty

good relationship with most presses and influencers now. I've got a lot of control over what gets shared. Media can be tough. If you hate it, we don't have to keep going. We can stop whenever you want."

He says it like it's a kindness and he's worried about me, but all I hear is that even if I say I want it to be real, it won't be real. He might try, but our relationship will always be dependent on how things play out in the media. That isn't a real relationship, and I think Ruben has been pretending so long that he doesn't even realize it.

Christmas Eve with him was magical. I want it back. But the two of us will never get our own little world like that again, and if I tell myself we can, it will break my heart when it all falls apart.

But I can't just leave either. Just like he couldn't give up the opportunity to have a relationship with Alyssa Fourtuna, I can't walk away from him. Not completely. If he's willing to be in my life for a few months, I'm going to take it. I guess I've been one of those women waiting for a turn with him all along.

I swallow hard. "Okay. Fake dating it is." I nod like this is a normal business conversation being held over a conference table, but I don't look him in the eye. And I can't see his reaction to what I've said. "But I have one condition. Ben has to know."

Ruben pauses before answering. "That we're dating? Andrew pretty much told him we were."

I finally look up at him. His face is schooled into an expression that matches my business-like tone. "That we aren't really dating. Otherwise it's going to break his heart when you go back to your supermodels."

His business face falters slightly. "Ah, yes. You have a point. He needs to know."

"So we have a deal?" I hold out my hand.

He eyes my hand and his jaw clenches. "We have a deal." My hand just sits there in the air, waiting. Ruben swallows hard, then leans forward. "But I don't shake hands with the women I fake date. If you've followed me at all on social media, you should know that." He grabs both of my calves and pulls them onto his legs. We're facing each other and my butt is still on the sofa, but all of my legs are now resting on his. He cups my chin in his hand and everything slows down. He slows down. With every inch he brings his face closer to mine, there's a clear question in his eyes. I know what he's doing. Giving me plenty of time to stop him. But he's the Alyssa Fourtuna of men, and I need to kiss him.

So instead of pulling away, I lean in. "Oh, I know. You always kiss the women you date for show. Why else would I agree to it?"

Ruben's lips turn into a wicked grin, and then they're covering mine, warm and soft. I've brought this puppy home and in one split second, it's already worth it. The hand holding my chin drops and slides around my waist to pull me closer until I'm almost in his lap. My chest burns with something all too real and needy—something that is going to break when this is all over. Instead of tapping it down, I relish it. I'm kissing Ruben and the rest of the women on the planet can rot in the prison of disappointment. Both of his arms are around me, and my body remembers his from the sofa last night. Ruben's chest rises and falls against mine, and the next time he takes a breath, my name is an unsteady whisper against my lips.

Something catches in my throat. As much as I want to tell myself it isn't true, he's not just Alyssa Fourtuna to me. I want so much more of him than his body.

And him whispering my name is too sweet. It's personal, not business.

There is no part of me that wants to pull away, though, so instead, I answer his sweetness by biting his lower lip. Softly. I don't want to hurt him, but it has the desired effect.

Instead of a soft whisper, Ruben makes a noise low in his throat. It wakes up a part of me that had been asleep since before the polar ice caps started melting. My arms are desperate with movement. I'm no longer satisfied with pictures of Ruben on my computer screen. I need to touch him, kiss him, hold him. I run my hands down his back, then back up to his shoulders. When I slide one hand down his arm, he flexes it ever so slightly.

I laugh against his lips and then pull away for a moment. "Making sure I notice all that time you spent at the gym, huh?"

His eyes look like they're on fire. "No one else notices."

"Liar."

"You made me think you had a baby, Cadence. I'm pretty sure I've got a lot of lies I can tell before I top that."

"True." I tip my head to one side. I shouldn't have said anything about his arm, because now we aren't kissing anymore, and I'm pretty sure I'd rather be kissing than talking. "Are you done kissing me already?"

"Yeah." He raises one shoulder like he's bored and chucks me off his lap. "In fact, next time we make a deal, we should probably just shake on it. After all those supermodels, kissing a girl from my hometown just doesn't quite measure up."

I land on my back in a heap, but push myself up on my elbows and narrow my gaze. There's a glint in his eye that I don't think even Andrew could catch on camera. "Are you lying to me again?"

His shoulders relax and he leans over me, placing each hand between my arms and my body. I sink deeper into this heavenly sectional with his weight. "Yes Cadence, I'm lying to you." He slides his hands under my back, pulls me up to him, and puts his lips back where they belong. On mine.

He's back to kissing me softly and I don't have the heart to turn his whispers into growls again. If I get hurt, I guess I get hurt. In the meantime, I'm going to concentrate on being the best fake girlfriend he's ever had. He's never going to want to replace me. Right now I think that means running my hands through his hair and running my lips slowly down his cheek and into the hollow of his neck.

He swallows hard in response and his fingers plunge into my back. Yeah, that was an excellent fake girlfriend move. I drag my lips to his ear and nip it, and then show him a few more of my moves.

They all work.

CHAPTER
SIXTEEN

Axley is asleep on the bed next to me in his new cuddle sleeper, but my head is still spinning with how much my world has changed in one twenty-four-hour period. After Ruben and I returned to tell our families we decided to fake date, the room had gone silent. We explained our reasoning a few times. I'm not sure Mom or Ben completely bought it, but eventually, for the sake of Christmas, we all decided to sleep on the decision before discussing it any longer. After that, it was like Christmas started all over again. We sang carols and drank Mom's spiced apple cider, and when the evening ended, Ruben gave me a kiss on the cheek in front of everyone.

While our kisses on the sectional felt more real than they had a right to, that little peck was awkward and forced, like we were trying to put on a show and the show bombed. Nobody in the press would buy a kiss like that. Andrew was probably shaking in his boots during it.

But the fact that Ruben couldn't pull off that kiss when he had managed to kiss all the other women he dated had me wondering if perhaps the kisses on the sectional were, to him... maybe...possibly...a little bit real? I pull an extra pillow to my chest and hug it tight. I'm such a goner. My feelings for Ruben have shifted so quickly, I think maybe I've been lying to myself all along about how I really felt about him.

I had a boyfriend in high school, so I don't think I could have started falling in love with him way back then, right? Maybe when I started my job at corporate? I'm not sure of anything anymore. Maybe in high school I'd just been too dumb to realize I could be in love with someone I'd been close to all my life. Maybe Moira was right, and I'd been chasing Ruben all along—just not in the way I'd thought.

The wall lights up above my silenced phone. My fake boyfriend/baby daddy, perhaps? I lean over to my nightstand, careful not to wake Axley. It's him.

One last present for you. Merry Christmas.

Dots are loading at the bottom of the screen and then a pic comes in.

My mouth goes dry. Immediately I'm scrambling to remember how to turn a picture into my screensaver.

Only the bottom half of his mouth is showing, because he had to make room for all those pecs and abs. The arm holding the phone in his selfie is so obviously flexed, this picture is for sure a joke. But, joke or not, the bulges on his upper arm are hard and defined. He's wearing jeans, but they hang low enough that I only see a glimpse of them at the bottom of the screen. I zoom in on his abs, because . . . well . . . okay, there's no excuse for it other than the fact that I'm as captivated by shirtless Ruben as the rest of the world.

He's flexing his abs too, but even if he hadn't, they would probably still look rock hard. Had I really been sleeping on those last night? And I *didn't* run my fingers up and down them? Couldn't I have had an arm spasm or something? I need to stop eating bananas so my potassium is low the next time I find myself in that position. The next time we make out, I'm adding sliding my fingers up the inside of his shirt to my list of moves. I'll even pretend like I'm doing it for his sake. I'm seriously the best fake girlfriend.

I pull my fingers away from the phone. I need to answer him or he's going to think I'm a little perv, drooling over his picture. But what do you say to someone who just sent you a skin picture as a joke?

Thank you?

I snort quietly and cover my mouth. Why am I so bad at this? People exchange pictures all the time while dating. There must be some form of protocol around it. But the few men I've dated for more than a month wouldn't have dared send me something like this. Well, that, and their pictures wouldn't have had the same effect.

But protocol doesn't really matter, because this isn't a boyfriend sending me a picture. This is Ruben teasing me because he knows I enjoy his football pictures.

Three little dots show up on my screen and I panic. I haven't responded or even liked the pic yet.

He's going to win this little game of chicken. I blast a reply before he can send whatever it was he was typing.

> You know how I am. If you get me a present, I won't be happy until I send one back. You're lucky I don't have to order this one on Amazon, or you would have been in breach of our previous agreement. Please hold while I get the lighting just right.

I quickly open my photos on my phone and find the perfect picture—one I took two days ago—and because I'm just the tiniest bit evil, I quickly save it as a file so he'll have to actually click on it to open it. While I'm doing that, a message comes in. In all caps, no less.

> THAT IS NOT WHY I SENT THAT. I WAS
> TRYING TO BE FUNNY.

I smile, send the file, and lean back in bed. So am I, Ruben. So am I.

One Christmas when I was eight, my mom ordered my presents online and warned me never to look on the front porch. I spent the month of December dying to open the door but never daring to. That is what I picture Ruben doing right now. Maybe he's pacing, or maybe his thumb is hovering over the file.

Or maybe he opened it immediately because he doesn't think receiving shirtless photos is a big deal at all. He probably gets tons of them every day.

Now I'm praying that he actually opens the file, because if he doesn't, he's going to think I'm one of those weirdo girls who doesn't know him at all, but wants him just for his goofy smile, great abs, and massive fortune.

But if he *does* open it, I totally win. Bragging rights pretty much forever. Ruben will have decided to open that picture, and I will 100% tease him about it. I mean, I have to have something to retort back at him if he ever brings up his skin pictures again, right?

My phone lights up.

> Why did you send it in a file?

> To make it easier for you to save onto your computer.

There's another long pause.

> So it's save-worthy?

> It might not be worth $100M, but it's definitely save-worthy.

So help me, Cadence, if you've sent me something naughty, I'm going to have to marry you, adopt Axley, and make grandpa proud.

I bet you say that to all the girls. Open the picture.

I slide out of bed, dash into my living room, and call him, because after that text, I'm pretty sure he's going to muster up the courage to click on the file, and I'd like to hear his reaction.

"Cadence?" His voice is a whisper, like we're misbehaving in gym class.

"Did you open it?"

"No. I have the distinct feeling that once I do, a bomb will go off in the living room or something."

I match his low tone, but add what I hope is the slightest hint of sultriness in my voice. "No bombs will go off."

"I don't think I'll open it."

"Scared?"

"You want me to open it."

"And you don't like to give your fake girlfriend what she wants? When did you become so mean-spirited?"

"About three minutes ago."

"Okay, then. I'll head to bed. You don't have to open it on my account. I wanted to hear your reaction to it, since there's a lot of skin involved. I'm not a professional photographer or anything, but I think I did a good job getting all the angles just right."

Ruben lets out a noise that's somewhere between a groan and a sigh. "I'm officially not opening it. Good night, Cadence."

"Good night, Ruben. I hope you sleep well." I can't keep the smile out of my voice.

I hang up the phone, grin at it for some reason I can't explain, and then scroll up for just a quick peek at Ruben's abs again. I shake my head and march back to the bedroom.

I can't fall asleep. I want to text Ruben, but that's ridiculous.

We aren't dating. We're barely rekindling our friendship. Well, that, and we kiss a little. Not complaining about it. Turns out I'm very comfortable kissing Ruben.

Forty-seven minutes later my phone lights up the wall again. I grab it, instantly wide awake.

> Very funny, Cadence. Thanks for keeping me up late.

I cover my mouth so my little squeal of delight doesn't wake Axley. I pull my blanket tight over my chest. He called me funny. Also, Axley looked absolutely adorable with his tummy rolls and dough boy arms in that picture. Ruben *should* thank me.

CHAPTER
SEVENTEEN

R uben picks me up on his way to work the next day. It's a short week because of the holiday, and typically half the office takes those days off to spend time with family. We could have done the same thing, but after convincing both our families that we know what we're doing, we're ripping the fake-dating bandaid off quickly to get the worst part over as soon as possible.

Ruben's Porsche Macan is nothing like a used minivan, which is the first comment I make when I sit down. Ruben shrugs. "I'm still looking for one with just the right amount of gum stuck to the seats."

I slide my hand down the creamy leather of my heated seat. It's only a five-minute walk to the office from my apartment, but I'm already dreading the day I don't have a preheated seat to drive me there. "I'm sure you'll find one. Until then, I guess we'll have to slum it in this pristine wreck of yours."

Ruben doesn't mention skin pictures or overstuffed sectionals, so we drive in silence until he parks in the corporate garage and turns to me. "Are you sure about this?"

"For the hundredth time, yes." I shrug one shoulder. "I'm dating Ruben Palmer now. No big deal."

His look makes it pretty clear he doesn't believe me. "What if I told you I'm not one hundred percent sure about it?"

"I'd say you're sane. Who fake dates? It is really weird."

"You know I do."

"Exactly."

He rubs a hand down his face and puts it back on the steering wheel. "Grandpa is barely okay with this."

"What did he say?"

"A lot of it doesn't bear repeating. But, basically, he thinks I'm no good for you."

I scoff. "He's been trying to get us together for ages."

"Exactly."

"Ah. So it's the fake part he doesn't like."

Ruben nods and then puts one hand up. "Don't worry. I told him not to get his hopes up, at which point he made a very strong case about not treating you like I did all those other girls."

"Did you treat them so badly?"

"I didn't think so. But you know how it looks on social media. I didn't realize he thought I was so irresponsible. Someday I'll tell him all about it, but he's going to flip out and make me stop, and I'm not ready to deal with that yet. Not until I know for sure that I'm done."

"Hey." I place a hand on his forearm. "Don't worry about Ben. We're going to be fine. It's just a little bit of fake dating. What could it hurt?"

He nods and gives me a smile, but it's short. "That's the thing. Grandpa's worried it could hurt us. A lot. And even our families' relationships. I just want you to know, all the things important to my grandpa are important to me, too. I'm going to be careful."

Ruben has been orchestrating his whole life very carefully since he was 15 years old. I have no doubt that he'll manage the two of us just fine. "Okay. I'll be careful too. Can we go in now? I just want to get this first part done."

He grabs the keys, throws them in his briefcase, and we walk to the elevator. The parking elevator is at the opposite end of the lobby from the main elevator, so once the door opens to the lobby and we enter together, everyone at work will believe the news articles.

The doors slide open and we're met with the five-story lobby bustling with employees arriving for the day.

My confidence from a few minutes ago evaporates and I freeze.

Ruben takes one look at my face and starts to reach for the "door close" button.

"No, I'm fine. Let's go," I say, but my feet won't move. When did I become such a chicken?

Ruben's chest expands, then he laces his fingers between mine like it's a habit, pulling me forward. His hand is warm, his touch gentle, and somehow my feet work again.

If we thought whispers of our names would echo through the lobby when the two of us walked in together after having a photo of us plastered all over the internet, well…we were right.

A few people take notice of us right away, and slowly, others around them turn to see what they're looking at. This is it. We're really doing this.

"Good morning, Howard." Ruben greets an older gentleman in middle management as we pass him. A few other people nod at us as we walk by, and when we step into the next elevator, a few brave souls join us.

Most of them are gone by the time we reach the 11th floor. Ruben drops my hand. "I'll see you after work," he says, then gives me a wink.

I step forward, my suddenly lonely hand hanging by my waist, and I give him a wave before stepping away.

Rebecca runs toward me the moment she sees me. "Oh my gosh, Cadence, is it true? Are you *really* dating Ruben Palmer?"

I smile, even though I hate that I still can't be honest with people. "He drove me to work this morning."

Rebecca squeals and grabs both of my hands. "No way."

"Yes, way." Oh my gosh, I've turned into a 1980's grunge movie character. "He rode the elevator with me, too." I turn back like I want to prove it to her and she laughs.

"I mean, no way that you're *dating him,* not that he drove you to work, you goose."

"No way, like you don't believe it? Or no way, like it's amazing?"

"I saw the picture. I wouldn't believe it if you said you weren't. But I'm shocked you never said anything."

Thank goodness. I was afraid I was going to have to resort to showing her the photo Ruben sent me as proof. Not that I would. He sent it to me, only. But I also kind of want to, because…hot dang, it's such a good photo. "We value our privacy," is all I say. Andrew taught me that one last night.

Both Christian and Mr. Auger are off today. I'm not sure if Christian is gone by choice or if he has already been "dealt with," but when I walk past his desk, it's bare. It seems Ruben didn't waste any time.

At lunchtime a company-wide email comes from Ruben. I can feel every other employee's eyes on me as we all read the message at the same time.

It's pretty straightforward. Ruben has talked to HR about our situation, and he'll no longer be involved in any of my projects. If anyone has any questions or concerns, they should feel free to contact HR to discuss them. He ends the email by saying Friday will be a half-day, and everyone can feel free to leave work at noon.

My face is burning.

I spend the rest of that day and Thursday answering questions about the two of us to pretty much everyone who knows me. I don't know if Ruben is dealing with the same issues, because he never comes to the 11th floor. By Friday, things settle down and I'm actually able to get some work done on the Laos proposal and a seaside Welsh location I'd been scouting.

I'm on my fourth day of fake dating Ruben Palmer, and if

you don't count Christmas, he hasn't kissed me once. Nor has he sent me any more photos. I'm beginning to think his talk with Ben basically made him reconsider any sort of messing around with Cadence Crane.

Ben is a sweet guy. I love him. But he's also kind of the worst.

Noon hits and everyone files out of the office. Friday feels like the kind of day a girl with a fake boyfriend should have a date planned, but Ruben hasn't said anything about going out. I'm not a pro at this, but Ruben seems to be making all the rules.

I hate whatever rule he has that means we haven't made out. But I love the one where he texts me every night. I'm basically living for those text conversations every evening, and I can't help but feel like he can only trust himself if we aren't in the same room. I should have chosen the real dating option. I've second- and third-guessed that decision seventeen times.

I pull out my phone and click on his name.

> Are you ready to go? Or are you still busy?

I tap my fingers on my desk as I wait for his reply. I could walk. It isn't snowing or anything. But I stopped wearing my sneakers, so I'd really rather catch a ride. Other than texting, I only get about six minutes in a car with him each day, and I don't want to give up half of them. My phone buzzes.

> I've got a few things I need to finish. I'll be ready to go in about 20 mins.

Twenty minutes. I blow out a puff of air and tap my pencil on my desk. I should be able to find something to do for twenty minutes. My phone vibrates again.

> Do you want to come up?

I stare at my phone and read his question again. In all the

time I've worked at Palmer Hotels, I've never been to the 15th floor or Ruben's office. My thumbs fly to my keys. Of course I want to come up. I want to come up so bad my feet have already started moving. *Sure!*

I sit back down in my chair and replace the exclamation point with a period. Now my answer looks totally nonchalant. Sure, I'll come to your office, Ruben. No, I won't imagine kissing you for the whole 20 minutes I'm there. Yes, I can behave myself in your presence. No, you don't have to keep avoiding me.

I force myself to pack up my things slowly. I'm not about to step foot into his office one minute after he invited me. I look at my watch. I'll wait here for at least five minutes before I go.

I wait a minute and a half.

CHAPTER
EIGHTEEN

I force my knock to sound casual—two raps. That's businesslike and not desperate, right? Ruben calls out to come in. He's sitting at his desk, his dark hair still perfect, and he doesn't look up from his computer when I walk in. I take a moment to survey his domain. Behind him is a wall of windows. If he was trying to make himself look like an angel with the afternoon sun glowing behind him, he's on the right track. His desk is sleek and modern, and a picture of his parents hangs on the wall. But my inspection stops when my eyes land on the black leather couch with deep cushions. The kind of couch two people could fall asleep on and actually be comfortable together. Or they could *not* fall asleep on it. Ruben catches my glance and the corners of his lips turn down. Something about that frown is my last straw. I stick my tongue out at him and march to the couch. I make a big show of sinking into it, kicking my feet up, and getting very comfortable.

"How's your work going?" I ask while sliding off my shoes.

His eyes go to my feet and I can't tell if I'm horrifying him because his couch cost a bazillion dollars or if he just finds me horrifying. He shakes his head, then looks back down at his desk. "I'm almost done. And then I've got a question for you."

I swing my feet down off of the couch and sit up straighter. Maybe I have a date after all. I'll play nicer.

Ruben is true to his word about getting his work done. He types away at some things and completely ignores me. Eventually my feet end up back on the couch and I close my eyes. I'm constantly a bit short on sleep, thanks to Axley, as well as Ruben's nightly texts. The leather on this couch is soft and supple, and I don't even blame Ruben for his frown. I'd frown at my feet on it too.

Time passes by faster with my eyes closed. It feels like only a few minutes have passed when I hear a scraping sound next to me. I jerk my head up to find Ruben dragging his office chair over to the couch. He stops and sits on it, a good five feet away.

I rub my eyes but don't sit up. "What's your question?" I ask with a yawn.

Ruben leans forward and puts his elbows on his knees. "Will you come with me to New York on Monday? Just the two of us?"

I sit up. "On New Year's Eve?"

"Yes. I have an exclusive party to attend with lots of social networking, and I'd love to bring you. Besides, I owe you a present."

"You don't owe me a present."

He narrows his eyes. "Are you saying that because you forgot to get me one? I gave you ample warning."

I smile. I do have one for him. "I'll figure something out. How did you end up without a date for New Year's Eve?"

He tips his head to one side. "I had a date. Oddly enough, Daphne broke it off when she found out I had a secret family,"

I slide my hand across the empty cushion next to me. It's an invitation, but I know Ruben won't take it. "I hear secret families are all the rage right now."

He grips the handles of his chair and the thought crosses my mind that maybe Ruben wouldn't mind kissing me again. "As they should be."

"I'll talk to my Mom, since she'll need to watch Axley."

Ruben gives me a tentative smile. "I hope you don't mind, but I already did. She was planning on bringing Axley to my grandpa's house for dinner on Monday anyway, and she said she could have Axley sleep at her place. We'll only be gone one night. We can sleep on the way home."

He won't sit next to me on a couch, but he'll fly to New York and back with me? This feels like the very definition of fake dating. "It sounds like you have everything figured out. Sure. Let's go."

"Great. Thank you, Cadence. I really appreciate it. All of it. Andrew says our romance is trending really well and this party is going to help solidify everything." I really don't want to say *you're welcome* to that little speech, so I say nothing. Ruben stands from his chair. "We could go early if you need to stop somewhere for a dress."

"I've got a dress. It's a good one. But I can have Andrew look at it to see if it meets his approval."

Ruben shakes his head. "As long as you're comfortable in it, it will be wonderful."

So I don't have a date for tonight, but at least I have a New Year's Eve date. It isn't a bad deal. But I really don't want to sit at home watching TV with Axley tonight. Or rather, I would be fine with that if Ruben joined us. Ruben just asked me to fly to New York with him. I can ask him over to watch a show.

"Would you like to come over tonight? Axley and I are watching *Friends* reruns and I'm just not sure he's catching all the jokes."

He glances at his desk and then back at me. "I was going to come back here after taking you home. I have some paperwork I really need to fill out."

"That's what you do on Friday nights? Paperwork?"

"Sometimes. It's what I have to do this Friday night, anyway. But trust me, I would much rather be watching *Friends* with you."

I think I believe him, but I'm not quite sure. I sigh and pry myself off his couch. "This New York party better be good," I say.

He doesn't answer, but at least he has the gumption to put his hand on the small of my back as we walk out of his office. Just before we get to the elevator, I turn to him. "I like the 15th floor. It has nice couches."

He gives me a funny look like he has no idea what I'm talking about. I just laugh. I'm doubly certain he hasn't been competing with me at all, and it turns out that the 15th floor is just a normal place that I could have come to at any point. Ruben probably would have let me in. Ben would have, for sure. I don't know why I thought I had to earn my way here, but I just didn't seem to care anymore.

I finally made it all the way to the top, and the only thing I could think about was kissing Ruben on those cloud-soft leather cushions. I think it's safe to say I've gotten over my inferiority complex. He can have all the big offices in the world. I just need the order number for that couch.

CHAPTER
NINETEEN

When Ruben said we would fly together to New York, I didn't realize he meant *on his private jet*.

"Are you sure this thing is safe?" I whisper in Ruben's ear. The plane is tiny, with only eight seats, all of which are equipped like little cubicles with desks. There's a pilot and a copilot, who introduced themselves before going into the cockpit, but no flight attendants, and we're the only passengers.

"I fly in it all the time."

"That isn't what I asked."

"Do you think Palmer Hotels would risk their moneymaker by flying him around in an unsafe aircraft?"

I screw my face to one side. "A valid point." I huff and plop myself down in one of the seats. It's way more comfortable than any airplane seat I've ever sat in, so I guess I can forgive the size of the aircraft.

There are drinks and snacks, as well as a hot dinner beside me in the cubicle. Ruben pulls out his computer. "There's Wi-Fi, if you need to work on anything."

"At the risk of disappointing my employer, I didn't bring any work to do on New Year's Eve."

He grimaces. "I have one thing I need to finish up, and then I promise I will be at least a little fun on this trip. It shouldn't take more than an hour."

"Take your time. I brought a book." I pull my *Dictionary of Difficult Words* out of my backpack and make a big show of opening it to the first page.

Ruben is already absorbed in whatever he's working on and doesn't notice.

Three pages in I hear him chuckle. I look up.

"*That's* the book you're reading?"

I shrug. "I read it most days. It's quite enlightening."

"Read any good words yet?"

"Acrophobia"

"Sounds almost like a fear of spiders, but I would never guess that. You would tease me for weeks."

"True, I would. And unless there are spiders on this plane, acrophobia has more to do with what we're doing now than arachnophobia."

"Fear of making an irrevocable mistake?"

I scrunch my face together at his reply. What do mistakes have to do with this trip? "Fear of heights."

"Ah, of course."

Ruben keeps his computer open, but every so often he asks about another hard word, and we guess definitions and make fun of each other's answers. The flight is five hours long, and he doesn't finish his one hour of work. Perhaps I should feel bad about that, but he's smiling more than I've seen him smile in the past three days, so I don't think either of us is disappointed.

When Ruben booked his table at the R Lounge overlooking Times Square, he also booked a room. He walks me to it and hands me the key card. "Is an hour enough time to get ready?"

"I haven't had an hour to get ready since Moira dropped off Axley. It's plenty of time."

"Great. I'll get ready in my friend Bernard's room. He's just down the hall."

"He won't think that's strange? That you aren't getting ready with me?"

"I told him that since this is our first official public outing, you wanted to surprise me. Apparently my secret girlfriend is sentimental like that."

"I'll make myself look good, then."

Ruben eyes slide down me. The motion is quick, not like his playboy perusal he used to tease me with. "You look amazing already." He gives me a short smile and then looks down the hall. "I'll see you in an hour."

An hour later I'm fastening a delicate gold chain around my neck and inspecting myself in the full-length mirror. My black silk dress hugs my body as if it was made for it. Because it was. This dress was one of my last splurges before I left Vietnam, and I wasn't certain I would ever have a use for it. From the front, it looks perfectly respectable. The straight wide neckline lands just below my collarbone and connects to inch thick straps wide on my shoulders. But from the back? Well, it pretty much doesn't have a back. When you order a dress to fit your body, it turns out the tailors can measure the lowest possible spot a dress can hit without showing your underwear. It is scandalous, and perfect for a ritzy New York New Year's Eve party.

It has only taken me six views of a YouTube tutorial to make my hair look somewhat close to what I'd envisioned. Ruben offered to hire a hairstylist, but I declined. With all the pictures that are certain to be taken tonight, maybe I shouldn't have, but what was done was done. My hair pulled to one side in loose curls looks pretty darn good. This get-up may just work as well as some of my moves on Ben's couch.

There are three business-like raps at my door. I open it.

Ruben is in a tux, looking very Ruben Palmer. His hair is styled perfectly, with just the right amount of shine, but instead of cinnamon, he smells like the cologne from his advertisements. He's as breathtaking as any of the locations I've scouted, and I one hundred percent agree with the rest of America. I'd stay in any room this man advertised. I motion for him to come in and say the first thing that pops into my head. "Will you please text me a picture of you in your tux later tonight?"

He laughs. "We're going to be together all night."

"Yeah, but not tomorrow, and I'm getting a little bored with your last picture." Not true, by the way. Not true at all. But I do limit the amount of time I spend staring at it. Otherwise I just start to feel voyeuristic. I wouldn't have to limit my time staring at him in a tux. "Let me grab my shoes."

I turn around and Ruben sucks in a sharp breath, then releases it right away. I set a hand on my hip and look at him over my shoulder. "Everything alright?"

He yanks his head up and makes a concerted effort to look me in the eyes. His right hand reaches for the doorframe and clamps down on it like he needs something to anchor him. "Yes. Everything is alright…great…ah…hunky dory." He grimaces after he says that one and I don't blame him. "I'm good."

His reaction is better than I could have imagined. "So you like my dress?"

"You know I like it." His eyes dip down for a brief glance and his fingers look like they might rip the doorframe right off the wall. "Now please put your shoes on so I can take you to a public place."

I sit on the bed and bend over to grab my black strappy sandals, then lift my left foot to put on the shoe. Here's the other thing about my dress. It has a slit directly on the side. Most of the time it doesn't show—not even while walking. But I'm not walking. I'm sitting on the edge of my bed with my leg elevated, so he's pretty much getting a view up to mid-thigh. I could have started with the other shoe, or turned so I was facing him, but I didn't. Maybe I'll send him a picture of me putting my shoes on when we text later tonight.

Ruben clears his throat. "I'll just wait outside."

"Are you sure? I may need some help with this." I lift the shoe like the straps are impossible.

Ruben clenches his jaw. "Please tell me you're joking."

I raise an eyebrow. "Do you want me to be joking?" Because I would let him help me put this shoe on.

"Cadence." He says my name like it's a plea. "I need you to be joking."

I smile. "Then I am. I'll meet you in the hallway in one minute. And I promise I'll keep my shoes on all night so I won't have to do this again."

The lounge is below us, and we're silent in the elevator on the way down. I eye the emergency keypad, but Ruben doesn't have a card to control this one. Too bad. I'd much rather spend the evening with Ruben in the elevator than getting to know his fancy friends.

Music pounds the second the doors open. The lounge has track lighting in multiple colors, and directly in front of us are floor to ceiling windows looking out over the crowds on Times Square.

Where am I, and where did real-life Cadence go?

Ruben steps forward, his palm warm against the skin of my lower back, and steers me into a different world.

CHAPTER
TWENTY

I hadn't realized I would be dancing so much, but it seems all of Ruben's friends had read about me online and were dying of curiosity. They were used to him bringing super-models, clothing designers, and actors, but a mom who worked a 9-to-5 job? Turns out I'm a novelty.

I'm dancing with Bernard, who's probably fifteen years my senior and has already mentioned two different ex-wives. His date is sitting at a tall table with Ruben and a few other women, one of whom is Daphne VanPelt. She arrived while I was on the dance floor and I haven't had a chance to meet her. I'm not looking forward to it. I smile at Bernard's date, but she doesn't smile back, which might have something to do with the fact that Bernard's hand has almost reached the spot where my dress starts back up again. If he goes even one inch lower, I'm either chopping off his fingers or stepping away from the dance before it ends.

Luckily for him, his hand stays put until the music stops. We walk back to the table together and Ruben jumps off the swanky bar stool and motions for me to take his seat. I've been dancing so much, I haven't had a chance to eat anything, but he's saved me a plate of fancy hors d'oeuvres and a glass of water. "Thank you," I say.

After I sit down, Ruben stays behind me, placing one hand on my shoulder.

Daphne VanPelt smiles at us. For a woman scorned, she certainly looks happy.

Because it was all fake, dummy.

"So lovely to meet you, Cadence. I'm Daphne, and I want to start by saying how sorry I am about that news article. I had a bad relationship last year with a boyfriend who *did* cheat on me, and my friends are really protective. They went berserk and I let our real relationship slip. I should've known the story would spread."

Daphne is so sincere and kind that I decide then and there to give up on the Daphne VanPelt nonsense. "No harm done, really. Right, Ruben?"

I turn so I can smile up at him. He nods and places a soft kiss on the nape of my neck. He starts to move away, then seems to think better of it and grazes the top of my shoulder with his lips as well. I grab his hand on my shoulder like my life depends on it. Or at least, like it might steady me so I don't fall off the barstool at the thrill of his touch.

While my heart is still adjusting to those whispered kisses, Amira—one of Ruben's romances from about two years ago—introduces herself. She didn't need to. I absolutely know her from her dancing skills online. Following Ruben when they were dating was extra fun, and I tell her as much. She laughs. "I was just telling Ruben how refreshing it is to see him with a woman he's actually in love with. I was so relieved when I found out about you two."

"Relieved?" I ask with a funny hitch in my voice. She just stated that Ruben is in love with me like it's a fact written in a textbook.

"Of course." Daphne lays an arm on Ruben's shoulder. "We both were. It's our cruel feminine pride. It's hard to accept the fact that the man we're spending our free time with isn't falling in love with us. I mean, we had agreed on a fake relationship, but…" Daphne shrugs and I know exactly what she means. His kiss on my shoulder illustrates the point perfectly. It felt *so* real.

Amira nods. "We never had a chance. And now, at least we know it isn't because we lacked charm."

I swallow hard. Ruben's hand is a firebrand against my skin. These women are both a lot more charming than I am, and they probably had similar thoughts to mine. *Maybe this could be real.* But it isn't. Ruben is simply very skilled at pretense.

Bernard reaches for a glass of champagne. "How did the two of you meet?"

We probably should have gone over questions like this in advance. I'd mentioned it once on the flight over, but Ruben had told me not to worry. We've known each other way too long to say something wrong.

"We've known each other all our lives," I say.

Daphne waves her hand in the air. "But when did you first know who you were going to be to each other?"

"Sophomore year of high school." Ruben steps closer to me, and suddenly my barstool has a backrest. A warm, tuxedo-wearing backrest.

"Yep," I say wistfully, trying to play along. I'm not sure why Ruben pulled that year out of his pocket, but at least I remember a few things from it. "The year our debate team took state."

"The year my *Teen Heartthrob* picture came out," Ruben says, and I'm almost certain it's the first time I've *ever* heard that magazine's name on his lips. His embarrassment about the picture seems gone, too.

Amira nods like that makes so much sense. "So you were able to lock him down before the world went crazy over him. Smart move."

It would have been a smart move, but I had been way too busy trying to beat Ruben. The thought of dating him had never really crossed my mind. "I wouldn't say I date Ruben because I'm smart."

"Why do you date him, then?" Daphne asks.

I can think of a thousand reasons why I would date Ruben, his selfie being one of them, but more than that, it's the way he looks out for everyone. The dictionary he bought me. The apple charm he bought Mom. But to say any of those things out loud would make me die of embarrassment. It would also be overkill. Ruben would never let me live it down. I crane my neck to look at him, hoping for help.

He saves me. "Probably because she knows she'll never have another man look at her the way I do."

Daphne and Amira nod. "That's legit," Daphne says.

"Plus," Ruben adds, because the man doesn't know how to quit when he's ahead. "She has photographic proof of it."

My neck starts to burn, and I know I must be turning red. Luckily, the lighting in here isn't great. If he makes me pull out that skin picture, I am sure it will be obvious how much I've looked at it. There's no way I can mask that kind of voyeurism.

"Ohhh, photographic evidence," Bernard says. "That sounds like a good story."

I place my hand over Ruben's. "No, Ruben, don't tell it. I'll die of embarrassment."

"We were in history class," he starts, and immediately I'm on high alert. He isn't telling the shirtless photo story. "No, actually, I think we need to go back to the night before history class."

I have zero clue what Ruben is talking about. If we were going to make up a story we should have made it up together. "It was our last debate tournament and our team all sat together at the awards ceremony. Cadence was wearing a white button-up shirt with black slacks, trying so hard to look grown up. But her hair was in two braids, and it spoiled the effect.

"She won the award for best speech and, thanks to that, our team made it to state. Everyone was hugging her and I realized I was going to get to hug her too. But when I came up to her, so excited to hug this girl I'd known my whole life, do you know what she did?"

Everyone shook their heads. I wanted to join them. "She stuck her tongue out at me."

"Burn," says Bernard.

But Ruben laughs. "Are you kidding me? I was delighted. I felt like I'd won because she'd been trying so hard to be grown up, but she could still be childish with me."

This story does sound vaguely familiar, but I'm not sure he's telling it right. "I'm not childish."

Ruben runs his thumb down my jaw line. I wish so badly I could see his face. "We were on the same team, Cadence. I was happy you'd done so well."

I'm not one to blush. Really, I'm not. But in this moment, my body is trying to. Ruben has me pegged and for the life of me I can't remember if this even happened. Well, except for my winning speech. That definitely happened.

"The next day in history class, Cadence had her hair in two braids again. We were getting our test results back, and guess who scored the highest?"

Daphne waves a hand at him. "We all know it was Cadence. Continue." Daphne winks at Ruben.

Ruben wags his finger at her in return. "I'd watched her get the test from the teacher, so I saw the moment she realized she had beaten every single person in that class. And after a little fist pump, she turned to me and did it again."

"Stuck her tongue out at you?" Daphne asks.

I feel Ruben nod behind me.

"And that's when you knew?" Amira asks like it's a totally believable story. I don't remember that test or the braids. I've stuck my tongue out at him plenty of times, but that's hardly a reason to fall in love with someone.

Ruben's voice is closer, and the hand on my shoulder squeezes. "My world shifted in that moment, and my heart opened up a space for her. No one else has ever come close to claiming it."

I want to throw an elbow into Ruben's side. No one is going to believe he fell in love with me because of that.

Bernard doesn't seem to be buying it either. "That's a great story, but what about the photographic evidence?"

"Oh, that?" Ruben leans forward and places another one of those soft kisses on my shoulder. It sends a shiver down my spine and I'm immediately transported back to Ben's den. Can you become an addict after one exposure to a drug? And if so, why wasn't I at least a tiny bit addictive for him?

Ruben rests his chin just above my ear and wraps both of his arms over my shoulders so he's crossing his arms over my collarbone and holding me in place. "Just at that pivotal moment—" His voice is low and everyone is leaning forward, trying to catch every word over the music. "When I realized exactly how I felt about Miss Cadence here, our school photographer stepped into the classroom and took a picture of me staring at her."

There's a very brief silence until Amira slaps her hand on the table. "Shut up." Her mouth turns into the tiniest of bows. "Your *Teen Heartthrob* picture?"

I feel Ruben nodding against my hair. "That's the one."

Daphne's smile is crooked. "So, you pretty much owe her everything?"

Ruben gives me a soft squeeze, and I know he's pretending. I *know* it. But I'm having a hard time breathing. "I won't disagree with that." I can hear the smile in his voice. What's worse, I know that smile. It's the *"this is all old news"* smile of a man who is confident and secure in his relationship. I make an attempt at the same comfortable smile but I don't think I'm pulling it off. This is fine. This is normal. Ruben and I talk like this every day. His words don't break my heart with their quiet devotion. Being wrapped in his arms isn't setting me on fire. It's such a common occurrence, it's like breathing. I keep that smile on my face, but something inside of me is cracking. I'm back in Ben's den answering a question very differently.

Real.

What would this evening be like if I'd said *real?* If I had, leaning back into him and feeling his warmth against my bare back might mean something more than just selling hotel suites and keeping followers. But I can't go back, and my smile isn't the only one that's fake. Nothing about our relationship is long term or devoted. I don't know how he thought to tie his Heart-throb picture to me, but it was brilliant, and both of the women listening are eating it up like it's the last cookie on the planet and they've only eaten kale for three weeks.

Ruben should have been an actor.

We're perfect. The cutest little wholesome couple they have ever seen. And then my heart breaks for another reason. Because Ruben *is* an actor. A dang good one. And after he admitted he was tired of it, I made him act one more time. So here he is, lying to his friends all over again.

We talk for another fifteen minutes, and all the while Ruben's arms hold me tight against him. The volume in the room starts to rise, like more and more people are talking over each other. When there's only a minute until midnight, everyone starts working their way to the windows to watch the ball drop. Amira and Daphne stand, and I reluctantly do the same. The air feels empty and cold against my skin without Ruben as a backrest.

Suddenly a wave of party-goers rush forward and I'm pulled to the left. Ruben's arm reaches for mine, but I just miss it. He's pulled away in the crowd.

"Ten." People shout in unison.

"Nine." I'm pressed between a socialite wearing too much perfume and a man that could use a bit more antiperspirant. I try to step toward where I saw Ruben last, but an even larger man pushes next to me.

"Eight."

"Seven."

I slide past the large man and someone grabs my hand from behind. My stomach flips and I turn, but it's Bernard. He smiles at me, but the last thing I want is to be with him when the ball drops. "Have you seen Ruben?" I yell.

He just shakes his head. "Three." I read his lips, because it's too loud to hear. He pulls me just a bit closer and I hope it's to protect me from strangers and not because he's hoping for a kiss.

"Two."

A hand wraps around my waist and turns me around. I let out a breath of relief. I would know the weight of that hand anywhere.

"One," Ruben says as our eyes meet. I've been dying to see Ruben's face ever since he told that crazy story to his friends. But now that I can, I'm grateful I wasn't forced to gaze lovingly into those stormy eyes as he told it. I'm not sure it would have felt like pretending.

Everyone is cheering, noisemakers going off way too close to my ears, but it all fades away the moment Ruben's lips touch mine. Ruben's kiss is quiet, like an evening at the lake, or the sound Axley makes right after he drifts off to sleep. It is soft and hesitant, like maybe he knows his story has undone me and he needs to be careful. His arm at my waist is firm, cradling me safely in the surrounding madness.

I lean forward and grab his lapel in one hand and brace myself with his elbow in the other. I don't want to be protected from the craziness that is Ruben's life. Just for this moment, can't I be a part of it instead?

Ruben's hand comes to my cheek, fingers splayed beneath my ear and jaw. He tips my chin upward, angling my mouth to make it more accessible. Then in a move that belongs in the movies, he dips his chin to bring us closer. I push aside the whispered warning that his touches are for show and let myself sink into him. If it's a show Ruben wants, I'm going to give it to him.

And I'll deal with him treating me like a business associate later.

His scent is musky and masculine, and as much as I love cinnamon, this fragrance smells like New York, private jets, and the slip of satin on the lapel I'm currently clutching in my right hand. I push his arm upward, and his fingers slide to the nape of my neck and find purchase there. This time I'm the one to angle my mouth to the side, and his response is electric. The arm around my waist no longer holds me safe from everyone else—it crushes me against him. His lips move possessively over mine. If Bernard would have stolen a kiss, this Ruben would have killed him for it. Ruben's fingertips tremble in my hair and his breathing matches mine. In an instant my body is on fire, a dry forest with no protection against him. If we keep this up much longer, the only thing left will be a pile of ash for Ruben to sweep up and take home as a trophy.

Not a bad way to go.

Ruben drags his lips along my cheek and murmurs something. I think it's my name, but the party is so loud I'm not sure. One firm hand slides up my spine, tucking me tighter against him, and then his mouth finds mine again.

As much as I've loved looking at Ruben's bare torso on my phone, being pressed into it, even with layers of clothing between us, is infinitely better. Looking at his picture is a solo experience, but these kisses are a team building exercise.

And Ruben and I make a very innovative and exceptional team. We should get a plaque on an office wall and a special parking spot.

A jolt hits me from behind. A couple similarly occupied pauses to apologize, and Ruben freezes. He swallows hard and then brings his lips to my ear. "Happy New Year, Cadence," he whispers, and somehow I make out every word.

I pull away from him and mouth the words back to him with a smile. But his face has changed. He has gone from spectacular boyfriend material to distant employer much faster than I would have thought possible. I don't think he hears my voice in this crowd. He hasn't had years of practiced listening like I have. I've looked for his picture in every magazine, listened in on every interview he gave, and pulled up his pictures when I was lonely for home.

I had thought it was Rosco I was looking for in those pictures, but it wasn't. It was Ruben. It was always Ruben, and now that I know my heart, he's going to shatter it without ever knowing it was his to break.

CHAPTER
TWENTY-ONE

S o I'm in love with Ruben Palmer. Big deal. Pretty much every woman on the planet is in love with him. It doesn't mean we get to *do* anything about it.

But as we reboard Ruben's plane, him whistling behind me while pulling both of our suitcases, I know I'm lying to myself. I'm not in love with Ruben Palmer, internet darling and king of killer abs. I'm in love with Ruben. The man who gave up any sense of normalcy so his parents could have it. The man who gave me a dictionary and hijacked an elevator so we could talk. And the man who just admitted that his dorky sophomore smile, which made the whole planet fall in love with him, was directed at me.

But I'm lying to myself about that too. He made up that cute little story to convince his friends that he could love a very average person like me. And although his plan worked, it had the unexpected consequence of making this particular average person realize exactly how she felt about him.

And the kiss that followed solidified every single feeling into granite.

The pilot and copilot greet me as soon as I step on the plane.

Six of the seats are still set up as desks, but the last two have been made into beds.

I'm not sure how I will ever fly coach again.

It's past two a.m., but after our bags are stowed away and the captains move into the cockpit, Ruben sits at one of the desks and pulls out his computer.

I stand awkwardly for a moment. I'm so tired I want to cry, and I'm not sure I can handle any more time with Ruben right now. I need a good night's sleep and roughly three years in Vietnam to recover from this evening.

Ruben, on the other hand, looks wide awake.

And very unaffected.

He opens his computer and turns to me. "I'm a few hours late, but I promised you a New Year's Eve present." He looks around like he's going to find a chair for me to sit by him, but all the seats in the airplane are very much attached to the floor. He stands and motions for me to sit in his seat.

"You really didn't have to. I thought you were joking."

He narrows his eyes. "Is that your way of trying to get out of getting me a present?"

"No." I sit and hook a thumb toward the cabinet. "Yours is in my bag."

A corner of his mouth lifts. "Good."

He leans over me, bombarding me with the return of his cinnamon pinecone scent after his shower. His fingers find the trackpad and hover on a file entitled "NYE Present."

"Is this another picture?" I ask before he can click on it.

"You wish." He clicks.

It's a report, and contrary to what Ruben just said, it does have a picture on it. I gasp the second I see it. "What's this?"

"It's a preliminary mock-up and location for a hotel on the Mekong River in the Luang Parbang region of Laos. It's been given the green light."

I don't know if it's the late hour or the fact that I'm emotionally drained, but tears start to form in my eyes, and I put my hand over my mouth to stop a cry from escaping.

Ruben sees it all. "What's wrong? Do you hate it?" I shake my head violently, but I can't speak. "I'm not working on the project. I just wanted to let you know it was green-lighted. It was going to be anyway, whether I gave it to you as a present or not."

I shake my head again. "No," I sniff and squeeze my eyes to keep them from leaking. This is so unprofessional. "That isn't it."

Ruben drops to his knees beside the seat and brushes my hair away from my face. "What's wrong, then?"

I turn to him, and the concern on his stupid face makes my lips quiver. I wipe away a sneaky bit of moisture from my cheek and try to cover my emotion with a laugh. It comes out all shaky. I sniff. "All I got you was a stupid fish."

Ruben's face lights up. "You got me the singing fish?'

I point to the cabinet that holds my bag with my chin. He jumps up and throws it open.

I close my eyes hard and concentrate, taking deep breaths. I'm not going to fall apart about this. "You can't get it out of my bag. It's hidden in the packing cube that also holds my underwear."

He stops and turns around, a wicked grin on the lips I was kissing just a few hours ago. "This present just keeps getting better. Can I request that all of my gifts be wrapped in under-wear from now on?"

Something inside me breaks. I can't do this anymore. I can't go from kissing Ruben one minute to joking with him the next. "Ruben, you *can't* say things like that to me."

His face falls. Gone is the Ruben that whistled his way up the ramp. I've killed him. "I'm sorry. You're right." He runs a hand through his hair. "I've gotten carried away again, just like at Grandpa's house, and tonight at mid—" He stops like it's painful for him. "You should probably go to bed."

"But what about your fish?"

He shrugs. "Well, I can't exactly go rifling about in your underwear packing cube, now can I?" His face is tinged red, and he sits down on one of the other chairs. "I'm not sure if I'm cut out for this fake dating, Cadence. I'm too prone to forget…And Ben would kill me if he saw how I kissed you tonight."

"You can blame the kiss on me." I force a smile. I'm not sure it's a convincing one, but it's a whole lot better than tears. "I pretty much froze when we had to tell how we fell in love, so kissing was the least I could do. It doesn't compete with the story you made up, though. That was epic."

Ruben's eyebrows furrow so deeply, it looks like a plow ran rows between them. His body stills for several heartbeats and then he shakes his head. A low sound—a laugh with no mirth—escapes his throat. "It wasn't made up, Cadence." His eyes are trained on the floor in front of him. "That happened. You're the reason I had that lovestruck look on my face. Why do you think I've always been so embarrassed by that picture?"

The air in the cabin is suddenly too thin to work properly, and maybe I'm getting dizzy and hearing things. I shake my head. "That can't be true."

"It's true. Ask Andrew."

"I will," I say with hands clenched so hard around the armrests I think I might break them. This makes no sense, whatsoever. He always wants me away from him. The pilot is making an announcement, but I don't hear it. I'm stuck in this weird space where the world isn't lining up rationally. I finally glance over at Ruben and he's doing the same thing I'd been doing. Staring forward, looking at nothing.

"Why did you send me to Vietnam?"

Ruben turns his head. "What?"

"If you've liked me since high school, why did you send me to Vietnam?"

"I didn't *send you* to Vietnam."

"Yes, you did. And you didn't write to me, not even once. Never even asked how I was doing. You visited Asia twice,

Japan and Thailand, and even then, you didn't check in or drop a note. I was alone and…" My voice starts to shake, and I hate it so much, I stop speaking.

Ruben hasn't moved. He watches me for a moment. "I didn't send you to Vietnam, and I did write to you. Twice. You never responded, and I thought that was proof enough."

"Proof of what?" I ask, even though I know I never got a single email or letter from him.

"That you asked to be transferred. That I'd made you uncomfortable."

"Where in the world would you have gotten that idea?"

"Stanley told me you asked for the transfer, and although he didn't say outright that it was because of me, he certainly implied it."

"Mr. Auger said you were making me uncomfortable?"

"Like I said, not exactly."

"Why would you believe something like that?"

He brings both of his hands to his forehead and rubs them down to his chin. "Because I could believe it. I know I watch you. That picture Andrew took is proof. I told that story tonight like it was romantic, but I've never felt that way. It isn't romantic if the person you're watching isn't interested. It's creepy. And three years ago, I thought you'd finally noticed, or other coworkers had noticed and started saying things to you about it."

"About you *watching* me?"

"I didn't think I was that obvious about it. But apparently I was wrong."

I'm so confused, I barely notice that the plane has started moving forward. "Let me see the emails."

"What?"

I stand up so he can have the seat by his computer again. "You said you wrote to me. Let me see the emails." I point both hands toward his empty seat.

One of his eyes narrows to a slit, but he shrugs and sits. He navigates away from my New Year's present and within a few clicks, he has an email open.

I quickly scan the message. It's friendly and curious about Vietnam. I would have loved to receive it. I look at the date. One week exactly after I landed there. Like he planned it that way. And that's when I see the problem.

"You're missing my middle initial."

"What?"

"In my email. When I moved to Vietnam, I had to get a new work email address, and they added the initial."

"Who said you had to change your email?"

"Mr.—" I stop.

"Auger." He finishes.

"Yes. Something about the domains there."

Ruben grabs the edge of the desk so tightly I think it might break. He closes his eyes and swallows hard. "I thought…" He shakes his head. He curses a few times, low and severe.

When I speak next, my voice is low. "He's the one who told me you wanted me transferred. He let me think that you hated my Redwoods project because Ben loved it so much."

He swears again and slams his computer closed. "When have I *ever* cared that you were better at something than me?"

It's true. If I've learned nothing else these past few weeks, I've learned that I was the only one competing. Mr. Auger must have seen my need to compare myself to Ruben and used it to his advantage. I took the bait, hook, line, and sinker. "I'm such an idiot."

"No. Stanley is a worthless piece of incompetence who couldn't handle the fact that a young new hire was outshining him. You were going to be up for a promotion if you'd stayed here, and he knew it." Ruben puts a hand on the back of his neck.

What? "Mr. Auger had told me moving to Vietnam would be the fastest way to get a promotion." Is everyone in that office pretending at something? "Ruben," my voice sounds odd, like I'm speaking through a long tube. "When was the first time you heard about my Mekong River idea?"

"A week and a half ago, after I talked you into coming back to work."

I shake my head. Mr. Auger had been filtering my emails the whole time I was in Vietnam. None of my ideas had been passed on to the committee. "That's why I was going to be sent back to Vietnam. He knew I was going to present my idea in a way that made it obvious he's been stopping my communication while I was gone."

"So you never wanted to leave Rosco?"

"No. There was a lot I loved about my time in Vietnam, but I didn't choose to go there. I thought you sent me away."

Ruben looks like he's been hit by a snowplow.

"We need to talk. This changes...everything." He grabs my arm and gently tugs me down.

I sink into his lap in a daze, the world suddenly making sense in a way I'd never thought possible—the air suddenly so breathable, I think too much oxygen is hitting my brain. He wraps his arms around my waist and I put one of mine around his neck. "Are you sure we need to talk? Because I'm feeling like maybe we can both just acknowledge that Mr. Auger was the bad guy and get back to fake kissing again."

Ruben narrows his eyes. "If this was a couch, I'd throw you again. Now, you listen to me, because there are some things we need to get straight."

I nod as if I'm a good little student. His jaw slides to the side like he might actually be debating my first offer. But then he clamps it closed. "When I heard you had returned home from Vietnam with a child, I didn't believe it. I couldn't believe it. But then I pulled up to your apartment, and there he was."

"But you know—"

"Yes," he interrupts me. "I know he isn't your child, but that isn't the point. The point is, I thought I'd missed my chance. I'd been waiting for years, standing on the sidelines, watching you and waiting, and while I wasn't looking, I thought you settled down with someone else."

"But I di—" My protest is stopped with a finger to my lips. I resist the urge to bite it. Barely.

"Do you know what it's like to be around you? You are a whirlwind—a tornado. You are full of ideas and passions and you're always going, going, going. The first time I thought about telling you how I felt was right before senior prom. I thought I would ask you to the dance, and one thing would lead to another, and you would maybe see me as something more than your competition. But then Garret Paisley asked you instead. You two ended up dating, and I cursed myself for missing my chance, but the moment you left for college you broke up with him."

"We were going to different colleges. It never would have worked."

"And how sad were you?"

I shrug. "Not much." His hand settles on top of my legs. It's heavy and warm, and it feels like he's trying to keep me here. Which is kind of crazy, because where else would I go? With every word out of Ruben's mouth, my world settles more into the space of this seat.

Ruben tightens his arm around my waist and tucks my head under his chin. "I hadn't missed my chance. Garret had. He got in your way before you were ready to take root."

I snuggle closer to him. "I'm not that bad, am I?"

I feel a low chuckle deep in his chest. "Why do you think your mom wants you to work at Palmer Hotels so badly? It isn't because she loves my family so much. We're just the only Fortune 500 company within 200 miles of Rosco and she wants to be a part of your life."

He might have a point there.

"I'm not willing to risk losing you again because I waited too long," Ruben says. "I don't know if you're ready for us. But I can't live through another moment thinking I've missed my chance. Not without asking you first to love me."

I bite my lip and close my eyes. Is Ruben really saying these things, or has the night of partying gone to my head? "So you don't want to fake kiss me?"

"Never."

"Because I really enjoyed those fake kisses."

He puts his hand under my chin and lifts me off of his chest so he can look me in the eye. When he speaks again, it's his cologne commercial voice. "*None* of them were fake."

It's time to be done with avoiding or teasing. When I smile at him, I know it's shaky, but his fingers under my chin aren't exactly steady either. "They weren't for me, either."

He closes his eyes, almost as if he's in pain. "Are you ready, then?"

He doesn't say what I should be ready for, but I know what he means. Ready for us. Ready to put everything aside if it means it will hurt us. So help me, I would even burn down that not-yet-built Laos hotel if it got in our way. I nod and press my forehead against his. "Maybe I should save your fish for later. I just thought of a different present for you."

"I'm a patient man. I can wait another week or so for that fish."

"Good." Warmth surrounds me like I've sunk into a hot bath, and I'm so comfortable in this bath, I never want to leave it. "Ruben, I love you." His hands tighten around my waist. "I think I've loved you for much longer than I realized. You've been watching me, but I've been chasing you, and not for the right reasons. I think I've just wanted to fit into your world, and I'm sorry it took a fake news story for me to realize it. My love is my gift."

His eyes are soft, not storming, but they still manage to flash. He tips his head to one side and smirks. "That's it?"

"What?" I push away from him and stick my tongue out. "That's a lot."

His eyes darken and he swallows hard. Who would have thought me being childish was attractive? "It's everything." He kisses the tip of my nose and shrugs. "I just thought you might also give me a kiss that I know is real."

I put on the biggest pout I can muster and groan. "Geez, fine."

But before I kiss him, I want one more good look at him. He looks tired and rumpled and just as sexy folded into this airplane seat as he ever looked in any of his photoshoots. And this man is mine. I will never have to buy another magazine in my life.

Ruben's eyes roam my face. "I wish I had a camera."

"Why?"

"Your smile looks like it belongs on the cover of *Teen Heartthrob*."

I laugh and finally bring my mouth down on his. He scoots me closer and pushes a button on the arm rest. The seat falls back with a jerk and I laugh against his lips. My laugh is cut short when his fingers thread through my hair and then nudge me into a deeper kiss. The plane juts forward on the runway and I sink into Ruben. Gravity tries to pull us back down to earth, but all it manages to do is crush us together. I'm forever ruined by the man beneath me. I will never be able to fly in a not-Ruben seat. This is the only way to travel.

We reach altitude before Ruben finally pulls his head to the side. I groan, because I am not ready to be a grown up yet. I've got about half a billion adolescent dreams to fulfill and he's interrupting them. But once his face comes into focus, I stop complaining. He's even more rumpled than when we boarded, but his eyes practically glow in the dim lighting. He takes a deep breath and I rise and fall with it. "I never thought it was possible," he says in my ear, "but you may have found a better present than a singing fish."

I snort. "You're only saying that because you know I have the singing fish in my suitcase."

"No." His teeth graze my earlobe in a soft bite. "No, I am not." And then he pulls my lips back to his to prove it.

CHAPTER
TWENTY-TWO

S pring has arrived, but there's still snow glistening in patches around the lake. I lean back into Ruben's chest and his arms come around me, locking together below my chin. Axley is probably ready to get out of his stroller, but we're only staying a minute or two longer before we have to head back into town to watch the second-to-last episode of *Broke or Billionaire*.

Episodes started airing weekly in January. Despite the ridiculous premise of one billionaire dating twenty women, half of which are wealthy and half of which come from humble backgrounds, it has pretty much taken the nation by storm. During episode three it came out that Ruben Palmer's girlfriend is Moira's stepsister, so the show and Moira went from being barely talked about to being on everyone's lips.

Ruben Palmer's fame strikes again. Everyone wants a piece of him, and I'm still a bit dazed by the fact that he's all mine. I cover his arms with my mittened hands and pull him closer.

"We should probably head down." Ruben's voice is low in my ear and his breath warms my cheek. Washington isn't cold when he holds me like this.

"I know. I'm just…"

"Preparing yourself?"

"Yes." Each week one or two of the women on the show leave, which means each week Moira will either continue living her dream, or she'll be kicked off the show. If she wins, I'm pretty sure she's expecting us to continue raising Axley. If she doesn't, I'm just not sure what will happen. Will she really not take Axley back after the excitement of the show has died down? And for the life of me, I don't know which outcome I want. No matter how much I love Axley, I know he must miss Moira, and no matter how fun it is to see Moira happy and living a cleaner, more fulfilling life, I can't watch the episodes without looking at Axley and thinking about everything she gave up.

Basically, I'm a wreck every Thursday evening.

I spin against Ruben until I'm facing him and bury my face in his neck. "Maybe we should just skip this week and read the recap."

"Is that really what you want?"

I want to scream yes, but Axley loves seeing his mom on TV, so instead I inhale deeply. Some perfume company should bottle up his scent of cinnamon and spice and sell it as cologne. They could call it TeenDream and it would sell out faster than Alyssa Fourtuna's new lingerie brand. "No. Let's head back."

Mom has our typical snacks laid out on my counter when we get back. I fix a plate for Axley, then take a seat practically on top of Ruben. He's my support human and he plays his part well.

"Mama!" Axley runs up to the screen and pats his chubby hand on Moira's face when it pops up during the intro. There are only three women left, and Andre takes all of them on a lavish date. Andre takes Moira on a helicopter ride to a mountaintop, where they eat a picnic and play in a stream. The only extravagance is the helicopter. Maybe Andre gets her.

She's going to win.

I hold my breath at the end of the episode when Andre gives what the internet has deemed 'the kiss of death' to a woman named Helen. I close my eyes and settle deep into Ruben's chest.

Next week, the finale will air live, and then the show will be over, so no matter what happens, at least I'll be able to chew Moira out in person soon.

The camera follows the rejected woman off the set, and then pans back to the three remaining people on the show. "And now, we're down to two women." The emcee's voice talks over the scene before there's a cut to him sitting in an opulent living room by himself. "We have one billionaire, Jessica, who also comes from a lavish background, and Moira, who doesn't have much more than a penny to her name. Or do we?"

The former boyband singer's eyebrow rises. "We have one last twist. One of our three stars has been lying all along about their wealth. But which one? And will love conquer all, when we finally answer the question *Broke or Billionaire*?"

Ruben's body stiffens and Mom gasps.

What just happened?

"What did he say?" Mom is the first to speak.

Ruben's body relaxes. "One of them is hiding their net worth."

"It isn't Moira," I say, even though it's obvious.

"It could be Andre." Mom says what we're all thinking. What if Moira did all this, gave up Axley, and then found out Andre is as penniless as she is?"

I shake my head. "No way."

"Do you think it would matter to her?" Ruben asks. "She seems to really like him."

I turn my head and look at him like he's crazy. "She went on the show thinking she was competing for the love of a billionaire. It matters to her."

"But maybe now that she knows him?" Ruben tries again.

"Oh, honey, that is sweet of you." I pat his arm. "But I'm not sure a few months of him dating her along with nineteen other women would make up for the fact that he lied to her this whole time."

"It could be Jessica," Mom says.

We all nod. It could be. But just like every other week, I don't even know what I want the truth to be. Axley has his hand in his mouth as he chews a peeled apple slice. Slobber is running down his hand and I just can't imagine my life without him anymore. "I don't think I can let her take him."

Ruben rubs a hand down my arm. "He's her son, Cadence."

"But she abandoned him. She just left him here. I can fight her."

"Do you want to?" he asks. The whole world thinks Axley is Ruben's son, and he's been the most tender and kindhearted father to him for the past few months. I know this must be killing him too. And Ben. Ben would be crushed if Axley left. His response when we got back from New York and told everyone we were done with fake dating was to produce adoption papers. Andrew, on the other hand, murmured something like, "I'm surprised it took you a whole week to figure that out."

Moira's face flashes on the screen as the credits roll. My phone starts pinging and I turn it off. Every week I get the same few texts from friends asking my feelings about the episode, and I just can't deal with it today. Mom and Ruben turn off their phones as well.

We sit in silence as we all try to process exactly what just happened. A sharp knock at the door makes us all jump. Mom stands up and then stops. "Do you want me to answer it?"

I have no idea who would be coming over, and the last thing I want to do is see anyone. I need a month to process this information, and I only have a week.

The pounding sounds again, and then the keypad starts beeping. My eyes meet Mom's, and then she rushes to the door.

It's Moira.

Before she can step in the room I jump up to stand between her and Axley. Her hair is wild and she looks like she hasn't slept in at least twenty-four hours. "Moira?"

Moira's eyes flash to mine and then to Axley behind me. Her

face crumples. "I've come to get Axley. I can't do it. I can't go through with it."

"What? The finale is next week."

"I know. I'm going to be in breach of contract. But I can't leave Axley behind forever. I just can't. I thought I could, but... now..." Her mouth quivers and she goes down on her knees, scooting toward Axley. She stops in front of me.

She knows she isn't getting him without my permission. After three months of being his mom, I have a say in his life now. And this is so typical of Moira. She can't even see a stupid reality TV show through to the end. No way am I letting her take Axley. But Axley has other ideas. He runs around my knees and puts his arms out. "Mama!"

Moira wraps Axley in her arms as tears well up in her eyes. She rubs the back of his head like he is the most precious thing in the world. Because he is.

"Are you here because you don't think you're going to win? Did Andre tell you he was picking Jessica?"

"No." Moira is resting her head on top of Axley's curls. "He was going to pick me."

"How do you know?"

Her eyes are like daggers. "I just know, alright? And I also know the moment that camera shows the two of us together, I won't have another chance to run away without people following me."

My stomach knots.

"So you're just going to take him?" Ruben speaks up from behind me. "When will you come back?"

Moira gives Ruben a watery smile. It has the look of both a greeting and an apology. "I don't know. People know Cadence and I are related. They'll come looking for me through her."

My fingernails dig into the palms of my hands and I step forward. "Are you telling me this is the last time I'm going to see Axley?"

"I thought you didn't want him."

I wonder if screaming would help. Everyone else has gone still. I clench my teeth together and speak through them. "Is this because you found out Andre isn't a billionaire?"

Moira's hand stops halfway down one of her strokes of Axley's head. "What are you talking about?"

"One of the three of you isn't what they said you are, and since we know you aren't rich, it's either Jessica or Andre who's lying."

Moira looks at the TV screen as if it holds answers. "But you don't know who?"

"No." Mom's voice is soft, like she's walked onto hallowed ground. "We're waiting for the finale like everyone else."

Moira's jumpy energy has vanished. She stands with Axley in her arms. Axley grabs both her cheeks and looks at me like he's found one of his lost toy trucks. "Mama!" he says again, proudly.

Moira gives Axley a distracted kiss. "What are people guessing? What does the internet say? Usually someone has some idea about a big twist like this."

I hear Ruben tapping on his phone behind me, and after a moment he clears his throat. "The majority think you're the one lying."

Moira curses.

I glance down at Axley pointedly. Has she forgotten a child is in the room? "Why does it matter?" I ask, my voice still hard.

"If he isn't a billionaire, how could I leave him?"

"What do you mean?" Mom asks.

"I just thought . . . well, he's Andre. He has the world at his fingertips. If I leave him, he'll be fine. But if he doesn't..."

"But what about Axley?" I feel like a broken record, saying a thought I've been thinking on repeat since I woke up this morning.

"I'm taking Axley, no matter what. But maybe Andre won't care as much if he's also been lying this whole time."

"So you're saying you hope he isn't a billionaire? I thought that was the whole reason for going on the show—to set you up for life."

"I didn't think I would have to win to do that. If nothing else, it could give me some exposure, and I could hopefully start working more regularly or sell stuff on social media. We've heard the show has been performing well, and I'm one of the last two women. I think my plan could have worked either way. Except for Axley."

"Cadence and Ruth need him now too, Moira." Ruben says. "They can't be mother and grandmother to someone for three months and then just have that ripped away." His voice goes soft. "You can't ask me and my family to do that either."

"We'll find ways to meet," Moira says. "I'll keep in touch. I promise."

A large shadow fills the entrance to my doorway. Moira had left the door open, and someone followed her in. The second he steps into the room, we all recognize his shoulder-length dark blond hair, the slight bump at the bridge of his nose, and his thick forearms.

"Andre?" Moira is the first to speak. Axley is wiggling like he's ready to be put down, but Moira clutches him closer to her chest. "What are you doing here? You're in breach of contract."

"Forget the contract, Moira. What are you doing here? Why did you run away?"

Moira ignores his question. "How did you find me?"

"I didn't. The production company did." Andre's slight French accent is just as fascinating in real life as it is on the show. "They have a contact with the media outlet that printed the picture of Ruben Palmer and your sister. They gave me this address."

I shake my head. I'm not going to be distracted by an accent. "That has to be illegal. Are they handing out my address to just anyone?"

Andre crosses both of his massive forearms across his chest. "I'm not just anyone." He says it like it's the most obvious thing in the world, and suddenly I'm pretty sure Jessica is the penniless one. "And Moira, you are the one in breach of contract."

"I'm not coming back, Andre."

"I don't care if you do. I can go on television live and tell everyone I choose you whether you're there or not. What I do care about is you leaving and not telling me where you went."

Moira's chin quivers. "I couldn't."

"Why?" The word leaves his mouth like a bark.

Moira swallows and then raises her chin. "I've been lying, Andre. To you, to the company, to everyone." Moira tucks Axleys' head into the crook of her neck. "Axley isn't Ruben and Cadence's baby, he's mine. And I thought maybe I could give him up, and just be happy with you for the rest of my life, but I can't. I would never be happy without him."

Andre's eyes fall to Axley. He steps forward. "And you didn't trust me enough to tell me any of this?"

Moira's eyes fill with tears.

I take a deep breath and stand next to Moira. "It isn't easy, you know. Raising a child on your own. There are so many emotions tied up into it. So many fears and uncertainties of knowing that one life depends solely on you. I got a small taste of that, but nothing like what Moira's gone through. If you love her at all, you need to let her make her own decisions." I put my hand on Moira's shoulder and the tears already formed in her eyes spill over.

Andre takes a step closer, he glances at me, but then his eyes rest on Moira. All of his hardness is gone. "All I'm asking is that you give us a chance. Don't run away. I'm not going to pretend this isn't a huge omission on your part. But it isn't like I've told the whole world all about myself either. We've been on camera for almost all of our relationship, for heaven's sake."

For the first time Moira's eyes fill with hope instead of tears. Her chin lifts. "Please tell me this means you're poor."

"What?" Andre asks, taken aback. "No."

Moira swears and then looks apologetically at Axley. "That would have made things a lot easier."

Andre slowly reaches out a hand and when Moira doesn't resist, he rests it on her cheek. "I have been poor, Moira. And I don't think it ever made my life easier."

A strangled laugh escapes Moira's lips. "I suppose that's true."

"Come back. Finish the finale. Something tells me the production company won't be angry about this secret. He's a small little guy after all, and already partially famous. We can work everything else out later. After the show."

Moira sniffs. "Unless you pick Jessica."

"Jessica is a nice woman. She isn't you." Andre says, like that's all the explanation Moira needs. And based on the way she falls into his arms, he's right.

I shut the door of Ruben's brand-new gum-free minivan behind me and look up at the tall pines surrounding his cabin. Moira wanted to put Axley to bed so after chatting with her and Andre for about an hour, during which Andre all but promised to buy a home in Rosco, Ruben and I left.

In one week, everything is going to change again, but I know we will weather it. "You know what the weirdest thing about us is?" I ask Ruben before he gets to the covered wrap-around porch of his cabin.

He tips his head to one side and waits for me to catch up with him. He's got to say something about how the whole world thinks Axley is our son, because, yeah, that is just messed up. But also, maybe he won't, because nothing about raising Axley together has been weird. He takes my hand and tugs me up the stairs. "Probably that you like sour cream and we still manage to make whatever this is between us work." He moves his hand back and forth between me and him like he's confused at how we ever got together.

I snort. I hadn't realized sour cream was a hold up for Ruben. "No, not that. I just think it's weird I ended up with an Edward. Me, the captain of the Team Jacob fan club, Washington chapter."

His eyebrows raise. "Is there really a Washington chapter for that?"

I shrug my shoulders. "I'm not sure, but if I make it up, I would be captain, right?"

"I wouldn't expect you to settle for anything less." He pulls me to the porch swing and throws a blanket over us. "I'm not one of those boyfriends who delights in saying this, but you're wrong. I'm not an Edward."

I kick my legs over his and use one of his huge outdoor cushions as a head rest against the side of the swing. "Like you even know what that means. And don't say you watched the movies, those barely count."

"You think I didn't read *Twilight?*"

My mouth gapes open. "You didn't."

He takes my hand in his and intertwines our fingers. "You were obsessed with them. Of course I did."

I'm trying to picture 17-year-old Ruben reading the series. Did he buy the books? Check them out at the library? Does he still have his copies? Would he give them to me for a present? Or maybe this is one of those lies he's been saving up. "If you've read them, first of all, how has this never come up? And secondly, how can you say you aren't an Edward? You are the epitome of an Edward—all shiny, rich and popular." I scrunch my face together when I say those last things like they're the most disgusting things on earth.

"No," Ruben shakes his head. "That's Ruben Palmer. I'm Jacob." He lifts a finger. "I've loved you forever even when all you wanted from me was friendship." A second finger goes up. "All I've ever wanted to do was make you happy." When he raises his third finger he leans in close. "And I would never, ever, drink your blood. I don't even want to."

I laugh. "Are you using my obsession against me?"

"Is it working?"

"Kind of."

He raises his eyebrows. "Only kind of?"

"Well, I've been debating confessing something to you for a while."

"Uh oh. That sounds serious."

"It is. And the funny thing is, and I'm not one of those girl-friends that delights in saying this, but you're right. You are a Jacob. I mean, minus the whole wolf part, which would be sexy, but…" I shrug. "Nobody's perfect."

He narrows his eyes and tips his head to one side. "Okay, is this thing you want to tell me is that you're leaving me for a wolf?"

"Do you know any available?"

"No. Werewolves don't exist, remember? And if they did, I'm pretty sure they'd all be in serious relationships. Sorry. You're stuck with me."

"Not a terrible fate."

"So what did you want to tell me?"

"Just that I love you, Ruben."

"I feel like you've said that before. Like every day. Lots of times a day. In person, by text, email, and phone even."

"Yes, but this time I have a *but*." Ruben's hand tightens on mine and it is the only indication I might have worried him. That isn't my intention, so I blurt out what I want to say. "I love you, Ruben, but I think I also might have a thing for Ruben Palmer. Like, I'm not saying I want to marry him or anything, but he's pretty hot. I don't mind being taken out to fancy dinners and riding in his jet and basically making half the world's population extremely jealous of me. I'm one hundred percent Team Jacob. But I wouldn't throw away a flier from a Team Edward fan club meeting. That's all."

Ruben's mouth tightens like he is trying to hold back a smile. "That's your big announcement?"

"Yes. Is that okay? I know you want me to think of you as just Ruben. But come on…Have you seen those muddy football pictures? Do you really expect me to give that up?"

"No, that's fine. As long as you let me keep braided-hair Cadence."

I quickly part my hair down the middle and braid both sides. I hold my hands out like I'm offering myself to him. "She's all yours."

Ruben's eyes go from walnut to ebony. He stands me up and kisses me, all while pulling me to the cabin door. His hand fumbles for the doorknob and when the door cracks open he stops. "Wait. You don't want to marry Ruben Palmer?"

I rub my fingernails through the short stubble on his cheeks. "Not unless I have to."

"Why would you have to?"

"I'm pretty sure Andrew is going to make me marry him when I marry you."

"Presumptuous woman." Ruben says with a smile. Then he pulls me into the cabin and kisses me against the door. "Thanks for loving all of me."

He says it like it's a gift. The old Cadence would have thrown that fact in his face and danced with the news that I'm ahead of him in gift giving. But this is the new Cadence, and I'm totally waiting until after he's done kissing me to do that.

WHAT TO READ NEXT

If you enjoyed One Small Secret, check out the next book in the Gift-Wrapped Romance series!

ACKNOWLEDGMENTS

I need to give a huge thanks to my family and friends who helped me not only write this book, but also manage all the other aspects of my life while writing it. Greg, Logan, Christian (who beat me at tennis and therefore wins a name in the book. I promise I double and triple checked that he was okay with the character) Vincent, and Everett, you are most important, even though sometimes it might feel like deadlines are. Thanks Kate Stoker for the caffeine, you always knew the days I needed it.

A special thanks to my beta readers, Anneka Walker (who dedicated her book to me, and so I'm totally losing this competition, you know, if I was like Cadence at all and competitive. Okay, fine. I'm totally like Cadence, but I hope not with my fellow authors.) Kasey Stockton, Mindy Strunk, and Mandy Biesinger (who had the most horrible week ever when I sent her my manuscript, but still managed to help me on one of my toughest problems, swearing.) Lisa Kendrick, you are fast and furious when I need you to be. The Rock would be lucky to have you. (Sorry, Joe. Also, I'm pretty sure I got the movie franchise wrong. But I still grant you the Rock, unless your tastes have changed recently.)

None of you will ever know the atrocious state of my grammar and spelling thanks to my two editors, Kim Dubois (who seriously always comes in clutch, I'm so spoiled) and Julianne Donaldson (who will probably retire from editing again after dealing with another book of mine. If you're keeping track, that is two books, two immediate retirements after said books.)

I also want to thank both the movies which inspired this novel. *Bachelor Mother* and *A Bundle of Joy*, if you haven't seen them, go watch them now. And please avoid comparing them to my book, because they are masterpieces and I don't need that kind of pressure.

I have to thank Heavenly Father for the chance to finish another book. I've got a lot going on (most of us do) and yet He seems to like sending more adventures my way. But that gives me more things to do with Him, so I'm grateful. You may get tired of hearing this from me, but every book is a miracle, and authors are some of the most fortunate people, because we get to see a miracle every time we finish another book.

And finally, a HUGE thanks to my launch team. You make me and my books feel and look fabulous. Writing a book is only the first part of getting it out into the world. Without you, thousands—heck, let's go crazy—millions of readers might have missed out on the chance to read this book, and that, my friends, would be a tragedy.

ABOUT THE AUTHOR

Esther Hatch grew up on a cherry orchard in rural Utah. After high school, she alternated living in Russia to teach children English and attending Brigham Young University in order to get a degree in archaeology. She began writing when one of her favorite authors invited her to join a critique group. The only catch was she had to be a writer. Not one to be left out of an opportunity to socialize and try something new; she started on her first novel that week. Visit her at estherhatch.com.

f **⊙**

Made in United States
North Haven, CT
03 August 2024

55703140R00131